DATE DUE

SEP 10 1997			
SEP 09 1998			
SEP			

D1126717

"Riker to Captain Webb. Riker to Webb."

"Riker, Webb here!" came a voice that crackled with static. "The *Gallant* had to leave orbit, but most of us are okay and accounted for. Find shelter, and await further orders."

"Yes, sir," answered Will. "La Forge is with me."

"Good. Is either of you seriously injured?"

"No, sir."

"Keep a low profile and await my orders. Webb out."

With a worried frown, Will picked up his trombone. "I guess it's dangerous in orbit, too."

Geordi looked around the ruined buildings. "Is this shelter? Should we just stay here, or go somewhere else?"

Will started to speak, but he was drowned out by a sizzling sound, like bacon frying. He and Geordi whirled around to see a neon green beam come slicing through the air. The beam plowed up debris like an invisible bulldozer. . . .

Star Trek: The Next Generation
STARFLEET ACADEMY

Star Trek: Deep Space Nine

Star Trek movie tie-in

StarTrek:
STARFLEET ACADEMY

Available from MINSTREL Books

STAR TREK
THE NEXT GENERATION®

STARFLEET ACADEMY® *#11*

CROSSFIRE

John Vornholt

A MINSTREL® BOOK

Published by POCKET BOOKS
New York   London   Toronto   Sydney   Tokyo   Singapore

A MINSTREL PAPERBACK *Original*

A Minstrel Book published by
POCKET BOOKS, a division of Simon & Schuster Inc.
1230 Avenue of the Americas, New York, NY 10020

STAR TREK is a Registered Trademark of Paramount Pictures

A VIACOM COMPANY

This book is published by Pocket Books, a division of Simon & Schuster Inc., under exclusive license from Paramount Pictures.

ISBN: 0-671-55305-4

First Minstrel Books printing December 1996

10 9 8 7 6 5 4 3 2 1

A MINSTREL BOOK and colophon are registered trademarks of Simon & Schuster Inc.

Cover art by Donato Giancola

Printed in the U.S.A.

To Nancy

STARFLEET TIMELINE

2264

The launch of Captain James T. Kirk's five-year mission, _U.S.S. Enterprise,_ NCC-1701.

2292

Alliance between the Klingon Empire and the Romulan Star Empire collapses.

2293

Colonel Worf, grandfather of Worf Rozhenko, defends Captain Kirk and Doctor McCoy at their trial for the murder of Klingon chancellor Gorkon.

Khitomer Peace Conference, Klingon Empire/Federation (_Star Trek VI_).

2323

Jean-Luc Picard enters Starfleet Academy's standard four-year program.

2328

The Cardassian Empire annexes the Bajoran homeworld.

2341

Data enters Starfleet Academy.

2342

Beverly Crusher (née Howard) enters Starfleet Academy Medical School, an eight-year program.

2346

Romulan massacre of Klingon outpost on Khitomer.

2351

In orbit around Bajor, the Cardassians construct a space station that they will later abandon.

2353

William T. Riker and Geordi La Forge enter Starfleet Academy.

2354

Deanna Troi enters Starfleet Academy.

2356

Tasha Yar enters Starfleet Academy.

2357

Worf Rozhenko enters Starfleet Academy.

2363

Captain Jean-Luc Picard assumes command of U.S.S. Enterprise, NCC-1701-D.

2367

Wesley Crusher enters Starfleet Academy.

An uneasy truce is signed between the Cardassians and the Federation.

Borg attack at Wolf 359; First Officer Lieutenant Commander Benjamin Sisko and his son, Jake, are among the survivors.

U.S.S. Enterprise-D defeats the Borg vessel in orbit around Earth.

2369

Commander Benjamin Sisko assumes command of Deep Space Nine in orbit over Bajor.

Source: Star Trek® Chronology / Michael Okuda and Denise Okuda

CHAPTER

1

Wheeee-skrich-do-waaaaaah! groaned the feedback from the Andorian hyperblat. Or maybe that was the instrument's natural sound, thought Geordi La Forge. It was hard to tell.

The blue-skinned Andorian smiled blissfully, and his antennae bobbed up and down as he played the strange instrument. The hyperblat was half electronics and half tiny bellows, and the Andorian looked as if he was strangling it. Finally he stopped playing, and Geordi opened his eyes.

"It is not in tune," explained the Andorian. "Perhaps another fortnight, after the humidity has fallen, it will sound better."

"What we really need is a *trombone* player," said Geordi, trying to let him down gently. "You see, the Starfleet Academy Band is modeled after a dance band from Earth's twentieth century. We play jazz, big band, blues—that sort of thing."

The Andorian sneered and looked around the barren rehearsal room. "Oh, you don't want any non-Terran instruments."

"Not true," said Geordi. "We've got plenty of non-Terran players and instruments, especially on percussion. You can substitute some instruments, but for jazz you *need* a trombone. And we lost ours."

The Andorian nodded sadly. "So I heard. Odd for a senior, only months away from graduation, to drop out of Starfleet Academy."

"It happens," said Lieutenant Commander Amelia Baxter, looking up from her notes. The stern, dark-haired woman was a tactical warfare instructor most of the time. She was also the assistant band director.

She looked with pity upon the earnest Andorian. "We're sorry, but the audition notice clearly said *trombone* players."

"I'll get one and learn it!" the Andorian declared. "Thank you, sir." He picked up his hyperblat and strode out the door.

"How many more?" asked Lieutenant Commander Baxter with a weary sigh.

Geordi checked his padd, a small handheld computer. "Only one more. What are we going to do if we don't find a trombone? How are we going to play that competition on Pacifica? Reassign the parts, or use a synthesizer?"

"That's not your problem, Cadet," said Baxter sharply. "You're the roadie—you just keep our equipment running. Besides, didn't you say we had more cadets to audition?"

"One more."

She waved imperiously. "Bring him in."

The first-year cadet hustled out of the rehearsal room into the hallway and looked around. Empty chairs lined the corridor of the arts building. There had been a tall, dark-haired cadet sitting in one of those chairs, but he was gone!

Geordi adjusted his VISOR to make sure it wasn't malfunctioning. No, the chairs were empty. Just his luck—their last hope had gotten impatient and split.

His shoulders slumped, Geordi headed back to the rehearsal room, dreading the look on Commander Baxter's face. Then he heard the titter of a girl's laughter, like a flute, and he followed the sound. Under a stairwell, he found the missing cadet leaning close to a young female cadet.

"You're up next," said Geordi.

The tall, dark-haired cadet ignored him, but the young woman smiled and backed away. "I have to get to class. See you around."

"Wait, wait!" called the tall cadet, but the woman was indeed in a hurry. He scowled at Geordi. "You could at least have let me get her name, or ask her out."

Geordi cleared his throat impatiently. He had always

been shy around girls, so if there was one thing he hated it was a ladies' man. This character was clearly one, or thought he was.

"Come on," he said sharply. "Commander Baxter is waiting."

He expected the cadet to be embarrassed, but instead the cheeky fellow whispered in his ear, "What does she like? What should I play for her?"

"Just play well, and she'll like it." Geordi glanced at the large trombone case in his hand. "At least you have the right instrument."

"My name is Will," said the tall cadet. "What's yours?"

"Geordi."

"Are you in the band?"

"Yes, but I'm not a musician."

As they strode into the rehearsal room, Geordi checked his padd. "Cadet Fourth Class William T. Riker," he announced.

Commander Baxter nodded wearily. "At ease, Cadet. In this room, I'm just the assistant band director. Have you ever auditioned for the Starfleet Academy Band before?"

"No," answered Will. "Am I supposed to audition before just the two of you?"

"Commander Baxter's back stiffened. "Yes."

"What about Captain Webb?"

Baxter bristled. "I can assure you, Captain Webb trusts my judgment, or I wouldn't be second in command. I should also tell you that it's very rare for a first-year cadet to make the band."

"So I've heard," said Will Riker with a cocky smile. "But you haven't heard me play yet."

"Then let's not delay." The commander motioned toward Geordi. "Mr. La Forge will accompany you. What do you wish to play?"

" 'Saint James Infirmary.' " The cadet glanced puzzledly at Geordi. "Where's your piano?"

Geordi picked up his computer padd. "I don't need a piano. My padd is connected by infrared to the sound system in this room, and its connected to the Academy computer. I can play just about any song, any key, any tempo. I can even pick your sidemen."

"Excuse me," said Will, "but I expected to be playing with *live* musicians, not some techie on a computer."

"You're not in the band yet!" snapped Geordi. "I suggest you *play,* or you'll never get in the band."

Commander Baxter smiled at that comment and looked expectantly at Cadet Riker. "You heard him. Geordi is our sound engineer, so he outranks you."

The tall cadet shrugged. "Okay, you said I could pick my sidemen. Can you give me the Benny Goodman band, circa 1932?"

Geordi nodded and tapped in some commands on his padd. "Of course. Are you going to play Jack Teagarden's part?"

"I'm going to try," said Will with a grin. "Key of A, and swing it, Mr. La Forge."

The techie tapped in another command. "Set to swing."

Will put his lips on the mouthpiece, worked the slide a few times, and blew some warm-up notes. Satisfied, he looked at Geordi, tapped his foot, and counted in time, "And a one-two-three-*four!*"

Geordi punched his padd, and Benny Goodman's wailing clarinet led the charge into the lowdown, bluesy number. Will lifted his trombone and blew soulfully. Maybe he didn't hit every note that Jack Teagarden hit on "Saint James Infirmary," but he hit most of them.

More importantly, William Riker had the right feel for jazz. He honked a few times and slipped off-key, but he never fell behind or lost his way. In fact, Will ended his trombone solo by putting down the horn and singing a few bars:

"Oh, I went down to Saint James Infirmary," he warbled in a pleasant baritone. "I saw my baby there. She was stretched out on a long white table, so sweet, so cold, so fair."

Geordi chuckled. Nobody ever said it was a happy song. After singing, Will nodded to Geordi, who brought the band to a rousing climax. The musician blared his final note and looked confidently at Commander Baxter.

The techie could see that Baxter was pleasantly surprised. Will wasn't as good as Leshelle, the player they had lost, but he would do. Especially with a major competition coming up, he would have to do.

Commander Baxter sighed, trying not to look too relieved. "You're a little rough around the edges, but I can see that you've been playing."

Will grinned. "I'm in, aren't I?"

Baxter rose to her feet and shook his hand. "Yes, Cadet, you're in. La Forge will give you the rehearsal and concert schedules, and get you the charts. You are free for a trip to Pacifica next week, aren't you?"

"Am I ever!" said Will.

"Don't miss any rehearsals," warned Commander Baxter as she headed out the door.

"Yes, sir!" called Will.

Geordi hadn't liked this brash, young cadet at first. But anyone who had so much fun playing a trombone couldn't be all bad.

He pointed to Will's horn and said, "There's an air leak around your bell lock. You'll hit those high notes better after I tighten it."

The tall cadet just stared at Geordi then at his trombone. "How did you know that?"

Geordi tapped the VISOR that stretched across his eyes. "I can see things you don't see, such as air temperatures and currents."

"You're a sound engineer—that's great," said Will.

Geordi smiled. "That's a fancy name for a roadie, and there are three of us. I love music, and I love machines—so this way I get to be around both of them."

"Not to mention the extra travel," said Will with a wink. "I'm looking forward to Pacifica. They say those beaches are something else."

"You'll be kept busy," warned Geordi.

"Hey, that trombone player who quit—Leshelle—is he still on campus?"

Geordi shrugged. "I don't know. Why do you want to know?"

"I want to ask him about his parts," said Will, "all

the stuff I'll be playing. He'll know the trouble spots, the pieces I'll have to work on. I saw your band play, and he was really good. You wouldn't think a Tellarite could play trombone like that."

"I suppose," said Geordi, "he might still be in his quarters, packing up. I'm not so sure that a guy who just quit the Academy is going to want visitors."

Will grabbed Geordi's arm. "Let's go see."

In the Antares wing of the dormitory quadrangle, Geordi and Will quickly found the quarters of ex-Cadet Leshelle. There were boxes piled in the corridor, and the door was open. As they drew closer, a huge shape filled the doorway.

It was the backside of the Tellarite, and he snorted his piglike snout at their approach. His hands were full of boxes, but he kicked a rear hoof at them. "Go away! You can't talk me out of quitting!"

"Easy there," said Will. "I'm *glad* you quit—I'm taking your place in the band."

"The band?" For the first time, the Tellarite turned to look at them. "Hey, I don't even know you."

"You know me," said Geordi, "from the band."

"Oh, hi," said the Tellarite, rubbing his orange hair in confusion. "Look, I've got to go."

"I'm playing your parts," insisted Riker. "What are the tough songs in the repertoire?"

Leshelle shrugged. "I always had trouble on 'Mood Indigo.' Too slow. Stand back, please." When the hefty Tellarite held out his beefy arms, Will and Geordi had to back off.

Geordi glanced at one of Leshelle's boxes and saw a peculiar symbol. It almost looked like the snout of a Tellarite's nose.

"Do you have to leave right now?" asked Will impatiently.

"Yes, my ship is waiting." Leshelle pulled a communicator out of his pocket and opened it. "Leshelle to the *Pakoos*. My luggage is in the corridor and ready to transport."

Geordi and Will jumped back even farther as sparkling nebulas of light swirled around the boxes. A second later, Leshelle's belongings had vanished in the transporter beams.

Will pressed on. "Which songs were you worried about for Pacifica?"

"Pacifica?" The Tellarite said the name of the planet as if awakened from a dream. Then he snorted and turned to Geordi. "You watch your backs on Pacifica. Strange things happen in that part of the galaxy."

"Sure," said Geordi, "we'll be careful. Why *are* you quitting?"

The Tellarite shook his head, tears filling his black eyes. "I didn't want to quit. But you know, blood is thicker than mud." Leshelle tapped his communicator. "Okay, you've gotten the luggage. Take me now."

In a sparkling column of light, the former cadet disappeared from the campus of Starfleet Academy. Will looked at Geordi and shrugged.

"Those were strange parting words," said Geordi. "What could possibly harm us on Pacifica?"

Will Riker gave him a sly smile. "Orion women?"

CHAPTER

2

It was a blustery night in San Francisco, and the air smelled like salt and seaweed. It buffeted Geordi as he walked across the commons, a big field in the center of the campus. He turned up the collar of his cadet jacket and stared straight ahead.

He was so busy just trying to walk upright that he didn't see the Deltan and the human until they bumped into him from each side.

"Hey, watch it," said Geordi, skidding to a stop. "What's the matter with you guys?"

"Sorry," said the Deltan female, a strapping young lady with a completely bald head. Akusta was one of their two percussionists, and she could beat those drums. "We want to talk to you before rehearsal."

"Yeah," said Stinson, a burly trumpet player. "About the new trombone. Spill the beans. Rumor has it he's just a baby."

Both Stinson and Akusta were upperclass cadets, and they never let the first-year cadets forget it. They weren't exactly bullies, but they enforced the upperclass pecking order in the band.

"Riker is good," said Geordi. "Not as good as Leshelle, but Leshelle is gone. I saw him leave. Unless you've got a trombone player in your hip pocket, I suggest you leave him alone. The competition is next week."

"I know that, frosh," snarled Stinson. He had a buzz haircut, which sometimes made him and Akusta look alike. "But we don't want a crybaby who's going to mess things up on Pacifica."

"He's not that type, believe me," said Geordi. "If anything, he'll probably be partying with you two."

Akusta smiled. She relished her reputation as the party animal of the band. "All right, we'll reserve judgment. But he will have to be tested. You won't tip him off, will you?"

Geordi sighed and shook his head. "No, I won't."

Even if he told Will, it wouldn't spare him from being the butt of some horrible practical joke—probably several practical jokes. It was a rookie thing, a long tradition in the band.

"And he'd better be good," warned Stinson, waving his trumpet case. He stalked off into a gust of wind.

"Geordi," whispered Akusta, "my tom-tom still has a broken lug."

"I'll get to it tonight," promised the roadie.

The statuesque Deltan gave him a wink and rushed off to join her comrade.

All eyes were on Will Riker as he entered the rehearsal hall, not early but right on time. The tall, dark-haired cadet, smiled at everyone, looking quite relaxed. Geordi lowered his wrench from Akusta's tom-tom drum and watched along with everyone else.

Akusta leaned over his shoulder and whispered, "You didn't tell me he was cute."

Geordi squinted through his VISOR. "Well, I wasn't sure."

"He is," she assured him. "And tall for a human."

Will made his way gracefully down the risers, through the chairs and music stands, toward the horn section. It was hard to walk gracefully holding a trombone case—he faltered only when Akusta caught his eye and stood up. Then he nearly tripped.

Geordi chuckled and went back to tightening the lug. "Now we'll see if he can play with distractions."

"Keep watching him," whispered Akusta.

That was an order, and Geordi looked up to see Stinson smiling at Will and pointing to Leshelle's old chair. The Tellarite had needed his space, and there was no one crowding the one-person trombone section.

Will smiled confidently at Stinson and nodded to a few of the others. Everyone was watching him now, and he knew it. He sunk his slim frame in.o the chair and hoisted the trombone case upon his lap.

The chair suddenly cracked into pieces and dumped Will on the floor! The cadet groaned, with the air knocked out of him. There was raucous laughter at his expense.

"That will teach the rookie to be late," said Akusta with satisfaction.

Looking terribly concerned, Stinson rushed to pick Will up from the wreckage of the chair. "You all right, friend? Hey, Leshelle was a big guy—he must have weakened that chair."

Will gasped a few times and finally brushed Stinson's hands away. "Where can I get another chair?" he demanded.

Stinson looked around the hall and shook his head sadly. "Aw, that's too bad—they're all taken. You'll have to go down the corridor to the auditorium."

Geordi stood up. "You can have mine."

Will waved to him, but he wasn't smiling anymore. Geordi gave up his own chair for the newest band member.

After that entrance, introductions were hardly necessary. But when Captain Webb and Commander Baxter showed up, they insisted upon introducing Cadet Riker to his fellow band members. Will didn't smile, he just nodded and sat down quickly.

There was one good thing about the trick with the broken chair, thought Geordi. It made Will Riker a little less cocky.

Captain Ulysses Webb was a portly sort, a chemistry

teacher when he wasn't conducting the band. The Starfleet Academy Band was his baby, and he came from a long tradition of dedicated band directors.

Still, Webb was patient and realized that he was directing young people, not professional musicians. If a cadet had trouble with a number, Webb would be likely to rewrite the part or drop the number rather than embarrass the player.

When discipline was needed, he would turn Amelia Baxter loose on them. Discipline was seldom a problem.

Rehearsal went very well. Will Riker not only played well, but he sight-read music. He broke off a few times when he lost his way, but he always got himself back on track. Webb stopped the band a few times, but it was never Will's fault alone.

When it was all over, Captain Webb thanked Will personally, which brought a brief smile to the cadet's sullen face.

"Are there any suggestions you would like to make?" asked Webb.

Will punched up the chart on the screen of his music stand. "This song here—I think I could play the solo on 'Stardust.' "

There was a loud gasp, and everyone gaped at Will Riker. Even Commander Baxter's mouth hung open. Geordi rolled his eyes under his VISOR.

"In your dreams," growled Stinson.

"Yeah!" came a chorus of agreement.

Captain Webb held up his hands to quiet the murmurs. "Mr. Riker, 'Stardust' is our signature tune—we play it to close every concert. The band selects the soloist in a secret vote. It's a tradition, hundreds of years old."

"He's new, sir!" piped Geordi, who never spoke up in rehearsal before now. All eyes turned to him as he explained, "He doesn't know about 'Stardust' or the other stuff. Give him a break—he's stepping in on short notice."

"Yes, let's forget it," said Captain Webb jovially. "Mr. Riker will have plenty of time to learn our traditions on the trip to Pacifica."

"I'm not sure I want to," muttered Will. Captain Webb didn't hear him, but Geordi did. With a flourish of his baton, Webb announced, "Band dismissed."

While the others filed out, talking excitedly about Pacifica, Will Riker swabbed the spit out of his mouthpiece. His sullen expression scared away a few people who looked as if they wanted to talk to him. After a few minutes, he was the only one left in the room, except for the roadies.

Geordi took a deep breath and walked over to the trombonist. "Great playing!"

"Yeah, sure, nobody appreciated it." He snapped open his case. "I just don't fit in here. It was a mistake."

"Listen, they're rough on everybody," said Geordi. "You're only a first-year cadet; you've got to take it. The thing you can't afford is to lose your temper."

"What did I do to them?" asked Will angrily. "I thought that in a jazz band there would be some camaraderie. But it's just more dumping on rookies."

Geordi shrugged. "Starfleet Academy isn't supposed to be easy. Getting used to upperclass cadets is sort of like getting used to the officers aboard ship who will outrank us. We'll have to take orders from people we don't know, people we may not even like. That's discipline."

Will gave him a curious look. "You talk as if you've been in Starfleet for years, but you're only a rookie, too."

"I was raised in Starfleet," said Geordi. "Both of my parents were in it, and I tagged along to their different posts. I guess I've seen how it works, so I know it *does* work."

Will Riker gazed down at his trombone. "I could have been raised in Starfleet, going from post to post. But my father liked his freedom too much, so he left me at home."

"Where is home?" asked Geordi.

"Alaska. I miss it." Will put his trombone in its case, snapped it shut, and stood up. "I don't think I can put up with a lot of broken chairs and weird traditions."

"The tradition with 'Stardust' isn't weird," answered Geordi. "You'll see. Besides, you can't quit the band until after we go to Pacifica."

That got a smile out of the tall trombonist. "Yeah, I suppose I can't. I'll keep thinking about that during rehearsals. By the way, my horn sounds great since you fixed the bell lock."

"Happy to be of service."

"See you tomorrow." Will grabbed his jacket and stalked out the door. He still looked angry about the broken chair. *Cadet Riker isn't perfect after all,* thought Geordi—*he has a temper.*

He had better learn to curb that temper if he wanted to make it in Starfleet.

CHAPTER

3

Like most bands, the Starfleet Academy Band had a touring bus—a Starfleet training cruiser named the *Gallant*. She was at least a hundred years old, some said older, but she could still make warp two. Her weapons and engines were outdated but kept finely tuned by countless cadets in training.

As he stood in a long line outside the transporter building, Geordi gazed into the cloudy sky. The *Gallant*'s crew of regular officers were probably running diagnostics.

The cadets would be put to work as ship's company to supplement the crew. Travel to exotic places and real-life duty aboard the *Gallant* were the best parts about being in the band. It was especially good for cadets who hadn't spent much time in space.

For Geordi, going into space was a trip home.

The line was moving slowly, a few steps at a time. They weren't even inside the building yet. For a big crowd like this, thought Geordi, there must be several vessels in orbit at the same time.

In front of him were the other two roadies from the band, a female Antosian named Murunda and a human male named Tucker. Both of them were studious cadets who went quietly about their business. But they were excited today.

Murunda bobbed on the balls of her feet. "I can't believe this day has finally come! Geordi, what are you going to do on Pacifica?"

The cadet grinned. "A popular thing on Pacifica is the forcefield roller coaster. It swings out over the ocean, and you swear you're going to plummet into the water. Then you streak through it and get all wet from the spray!"

"Have you been there?" asked Tucker with amazement. He was a stocky young man from Arkansas, and sometimes his slow drawl fooled people into thinking he was all muscles and no brains. But he had helped tutor Geordi in quantum mechanics.

"Yeah," said Geordi, trying not to sound surprised that Tucker hadn't been there. "With my parents."

Before they could pump him for more information about Pacifica, Will Riker joined them at the end of the line. "Hi, Geordi, Murunda, Tucker."

They all greeted the newest member of the band.

18

"You know," said Tucker, "you could go to the head of the line if you wanted. The transporter chief has orders to beam up the musicians first."

"You don't have to hang out with us," Murunda explained.

Will scowled. "I'm allowed to pick my own friends, aren't I? What is this, another silly tradition? Besides, there's none of them I want to hang out with."

Just then the stunning Deltan, Akusta, walked past on her way to the head of the line. She stopped and craned her long, graceful neck toward Will. "Riker, you don't have to wait in line. Come along."

The trombonist blinked in surprise, then looked apologetically at the roadies.

"Go ahead," said Geordi with a smile.

"I'll catch up with you later," promised Will, as he hurried off to join Akusta.

"It's not going to be easy to keep that boy out of trouble," said Murunda.

Geordi sighed. "I'm afraid you're right."

A few minutes later, they finally reached the doorway of the transporter building. Geordi stepped under a gleaming arch, and a blast of air hit him and whisked the street dirt outside. Ultraviolet lights killed a few more microbes, and the biofilter in the transporter would get the rest.

He hefted his duffel bag and waited to step aboard the transporter platform. A lieutenant asked their names and checked them off his roster. Then the transporter chief checked his controls and ordered them onto the platform.

As they settled into place on the lighted pads, Geordi looked at his fellow roadies and smiled. Until a person had transported a zillion times, it was an odd and scary feeling. Geordi had already transported a zillion times, and this was no stranger to him than a walk on the commons.

When the lieutenant said, "Energize," both Murunda and Tucker screwed their eyes shut. Geordi kept his eyes open and watched as the room on Earth faded away—to be replaced by the sterile transporter room of the *Gallant*.

He filled his lungs with recycled air and noted that it was warmer and dryer than San Francisco's. Geordi felt right at home.

Another lieutenant motioned to them from the doorway and led them into a briefing room. He checked them in on his padd and issued them comm badges, work assignments, and bunk assignments. Now they were officially ship's company!

On the way to Pacifica, the work assignments were only half shifts, to give the band plenty of time to rehearse. On the way back, they would be full shifts. Geordi was pleased to find that he was assigned to Engineering, and his shift began immediately.

Murunda was headed to the bridge but not until much later, and Tucker had a security detail, also later. The big human always drew security, whether he wanted it or not.

The bunk assignments were cut-and-dried, women in one dorm and men in the other. The old-fashioned cruiser had old-fashioned dormitories, with only a handful of private quarters for the command crew.

Geordi walked with Murunda and Tucker to the dormitories, but he didn't go in. He stashed his bag in a locker, said good-bye to his friends, and headed to Engineering on deck 8.

When Geordi exited from the turbolift, he realized that he had taken the forward lift instead of the aft lift. He scowled at his own stupidity. Instead of being right at engineering, he had to backtrack several dreary corridors on deck 8 to get there.

Geordi was strolling toward the intersection of two corridors, when he saw a very strange sight. A naked man dashed through the intersection and disappeared!

Geordi stopped and pondered what he had seen. He looked around, but there was nobody else in the corridor to verify what he had seen. Perhaps the figure wasn't naked, but he didn't have very many clothes on. In the Engineering section of a Starfleet vessel, that was a rare sight.

The cadet continued his walk down the corridor, more slowly. Sure enough, as he passed through the intersection, he spotted an open hatch that shouldn't be open. Geordi touched his commbadge, wondering if he should alert security.

What was he going to tell them? wondered Geordi. That he had seen a naked man? Perhaps he had better make certain of what he saw before he reported it.

The cadet pressed against the bulkhead across from the open hatch, careful not to get too close. His hand was only a few centimeters away from his commbadge, ready to alert security.

He stared into the darkness of a small storage room.

This was one part of the *Gallant* that looked all of its one hundred years.

"Is there anybody in there?" he asked in a stern voice.

"Geordi!" came a surprised whisper. "Is that you?"

"Will?"

Slowly, Cadet Riker emerged from the storage room. Geordi could see that he was wearing nothing but a bathing suit, and he burst out laughing.

"Ssshhh!" hissed Will. "Do you want to get me caught?"

Geordi pressed his hand to his mouth and tried to control his laughter. "What are you doing down here in a bathing suit? The showers are five decks above us."

"I'm lost. And cold." Will wrapped his arms around his bare shoulders and shivered. Whether it was from cold or embarrassment, it was hard to tell.

Geordi tried hard to keep a smile from sneaking across his face. "I'm supposed to report to Engineering. If you want me to help you, you'd better tell me how you got here like this."

Will sunk into the darkness of the storage room and began his story: "You see, Akusta and I didn't have to report to our duty assignments until tonight. So she suggested we go swimming. . . ."

Despite his best intentions, Geordi burst out laughing again.

Angrily Will continued. "I had my bathing suit for Pacifica, and Akusta said there was a swimming pool on board. So we grabbed our suits. I followed her from one end of the ship to the other until finally we came to a place she said was the changing room."

As Geordi started chuckling again, Will glared at him. "Anyway, she had to leave the room to change into her bathing suit. She told me that I could change, leave my clothes in there, and walk through a door to the pool. So I changed, and I was on my way to the pool. Or so I thought."

Will shook his head in amazement. "I walked into sickbay, where everybody started laughing at me. Then I rushed back to get my uniform, and it was gone! After that, I just ran for it. So here I am, stranded somewhere on the *Gallant*—in my bathing suit!"

Geordi had to remove his VISOR to rub his eyes. "I've never liked practical jokes, but this is a good one."

The embarrassed cadet frowned. "Maybe for *you* it's a good one. I've got to get some clothes on before Webb or Baxter sees me like this. Akusta must have stolen my uniform."

"Listen," said Geordi, "if I remember correctly, there are some laboratories around here. Let me see if I can get you a lab smock or something. Stay here."

Geordi rushed off down the corridor, shaking his head at Will's predicament. The musician was lucky that he had run into a friend who was willing to help him. They would have to be lucky to get him back to his bunk without being seen.

Geordi spied a door marked Supplies. That could be anything, but maybe it was lab supplies. He noticed that the lock was controlled by voice identification, so he cleared his throat and announced himself.

"Cadet La Forge requests permission to enter."

"Authorization code?" asked the computer.

Geordi shook his head. "Uh, I don't have an authorization code."

"Access denied."

Without thinking he touched the door. At once sirens went off in the corridor, and the computer shouted, "Unauthorized access in progress! Unauthorized access in progress!"

Geordi hopped back and waved his hands at the deafening door. "Be quiet! It's no big deal!"

Will Riker came rushing into the corridor. "What's going on?" His bare feet slipped on the deck, and he fell on his rear end and slid into the bulkhead.

As if things couldn't get any worse, Commander Baxter came charging down the other end of the corridor. Right behind her was a security detail composed mostly of cadets. In the front was Stinson, and he roared with laughter when he saw Will lying on his back in his bathing suit.

Commander Baxter looked down at the embarrassed cadet. "Riker, you're out of uniform."

"Yes, sir," said Will. He scrambled to his feet and rubbed his tailbone. "I, uh . . . I don't know where it is."

The other cadets burst out laughing, and Baxter shot them a glare. Then she turned back to Will. "Who set off the alarm?"

"That was me, sir," muttered Geordi. "I was just trying to find him something to wear."

Baxter scowled and took the padd off her belt. She punched in some commands. "You should have reported him, Mr. La Forge. Because of this incident, I've changed both of your work assignments to cafeteria duty. Mr. Riker, would you like to tell me who led you down here?"

Riker thought about it for a moment. "I was at fault, sir."

A slight smile crept over Baxter's face. "In the future, I hope you will remember that there is no swimming pool on the *Gallant.*"

"Will's shoulders slumped. "Yes, sir."

"Both of you, report to the cafeteria," the captain ordered. "First, go to the supply replicator on deck three, where Mr. Riker can get a new uniform. Dismissed."

As Will and Geordi walked away, the captain called after them, "Remember the rehearsal at fourteen-hundred hours."

Geordi and Will picked up their pace as they hurried away from the others. They ducked into the turbolift and Geordi ordered "Deck three."

"As soon as this trip is over," muttered Will, "I'm quitting this stupid band."

"What are you complaining about?" growled Geordi. "I lost my turn in Engineering because of you! I may never get to spend time in Engineering again."

"Give me a break," groaned Will. "I audition for the band, make it, and everybody treats me like dirt."

"Do I treat you like dirt?" Geordi stared up at the taller man, but then he realized that Will was standing in a Starfleet turbolift in his bathing suit! He burst out laughing.

Will Riker couldn't help smile. "Oh, shut up."

CHAPTER

4

After three days of scraping dirty dishes, nobody was happier to see Pacifica than Geordi and Will. They gazed at the gleaming turquoise planet through the small window in the cafeteria. Thousands of islands dotted the vast ocean like flower petals on a lake.

Riker started to untie his apron. "We made it! Those beaches are calling my name."

"Wait a minute," warned Geordi. "We've got to wait for orders."

A voice broke over the ship's intercom. "This is Captain Webb to all cadets with the Starfleet Academy Band. You are relieved of shipboard duty. Pack up, put on your dress uniforms, and report to transporter room one. Remember to keep your comm-badges. Webb out."

Now Geordi and Will raced each other to get out of their aprons and into the turbolift. When they reached the men's dormitory, several members of the band were already changing out of their cadet jumpsuits into their gray and white dress uniforms.

"Hey, Riker!" called Stinson. "Don't forget to bring your bathing suit!"

There was a round of laughter, and Will shook his head. "I'll never live that down, will I?"

"No," answered Stinson. "But you had a chance to rat on Akusta, and you didn't do it. That's one point in your favor. That, and the fact that you can play some trombone."

"Thanks," grumbled Will.

Geordi smiled to himself, thinking that Will might not want to quit the band if he had a great time on Pacifica. Even if they didn't win the competition, there would be plenty of fun. Even kitchen duty couldn't spoil this trip. Nothing could spoil it.

Then he saw the box at the foot of his bunk, and he frowned. It was a sleek, oval-shaped device with a circle of colored buttons on the top. He wondered if he would be able to fit it into his duffel bag.

"Darn it," he said. "I forgot to put this with the rest of the equipment. Now I'll have to carry it in my luggage."

"What is it?" asked Riker.

"A Coridan phase modulator." Geordi shook his head. "Many years ago there was a Coridan in the band, and he gave this to Captain Webb when he left. The captain has been looking for someone to play it ever since. I can't even get it *working,* and we need it for the train whistle effect on 'Take the A Train.' "

Riker smiled. "I like it when the horn section just shouts, 'Wooo-wooo!' "

"You would. But this gizmo also doubles on guitar and harp. It adds a nice quality to the band's sound— at least, that's what Captain Webb says. Anyway, I'll have to fix it later."

Somehow Geordi stuffed the alien instrument into his duffel bag along with his personal belongings. Then he transferred his commbadge to his dress uniform.

Everyone else was filing out of the room, and Will turned to Geordi. "Ready?"

"Ready."

Like everyone else, Geordi was excited. Pacifica was the jewel of the Federation, a paradise open to all, and a haven for weary travelers. Operating under a Federation governor, it was the perfect place for conferences, competitions, or just plain relaxing.

When they got to the transporter room of the *Gallant,* Captain Webb was personally checking names. "La Forge and Riker," he said as they filed past. "Do you mind rooming together?"

"No, sir," they both answered.

The portly band director handed them small cards. "Your room is 294 on the Terrace Gardens. The cards will unlock your door and also cover meals and transportation. Don't forget, be at Titan Hall at nineteen-hundred hours for our performance."

"Yes, sir," they answered. Grinning happily, the two young men took their places on the transporter pads.

Webb nodded, then remembered something. "Mr. La Forge, how are you doing with the phase modulator?"

Geordi frowned. "It's still giving me problems. I'm not sure it will be ready by tonight."

"Well, keep working on it," ordered Webb. "We don't want the horn section to have to yell 'Wooo-wooo.' "

"No, sir," said Geordi glumly. Will gave him a smile.

"Energize," said Captain Webb.

A moment later, the dull transporter room of the *Gallant* faded away, and they found themselves in a beautiful garden. At first Geordi thought they were outdoors. Then he realized there was a clear dome over their heads. The ceiling was so high that gigantic purple trees brushed the top of it.

Outside the garden was a golden beach that shimmered in the light of two suns. The older sun was blood red and hung low over the horizon. The newer sun was gleaming white and hung high in the sky. Beyond the beach, turquoise water stretched as far as the eye could see, and a flock of scarlet and yellow birds flew past.

With his mouth hanging open, Will Riker stepped off the transporter platform. Other young people from all over the Federation were arriving on other transporter platforms in the garden. Will didn't know which to look at first—the beautiful scenery or the young women.

"This is more like it," he said.

"Yeah," agreed Geordi. "Do you want to find our room?"

Just then, four young ladies with pink hair walked past, and one of them smiled at Will. He handed Geordi his duffel bag. "You find the room. I'm going to see the sights."

"What about getting something to eat?" asked Geordi.

But Will was already running to catch up with the pink-haired women. Geordi shook his head and sighed. "Enjoy the sights."

Lugging both their bags, Geordi walked out of the dome and across a bridge spanning two islands. He looked down into the turquoise water to see a school of sleek orange fish gliding along. Overhead, the purple trees swayed gently in the breeze, and he heard the sound of laughter from the beach.

Starfleet Academy was close to the ocean, but that ocean was cold and gray. This one was warm and gentle. Thanks to Pacifica's two suns, there were always long days and long sunsets. At night there was only one hour of darkness, so there was plenty of time for fun.

Geordi passed a bench and decided to sit down. He gazed at the golden beach, where people were swimming, sunbathing, and flying small discs across the sand. It didn't look as if anyone had a care in the world, except for Geordi. He had to get the stupid phase modulator working by 1900 hours.

He was getting nervous about the performance. If the judges liked them today, they would get to perform tomorrow in the finals. If they did well in the competition, they might get invited to play in other exotic places.

Might as well start working on the modulator, Geordi told himself. He took the device out of his duffel bag, turned it on, and tried a few of the keys. Nothing happened. It was as dead as a moon rock.

Just then, a group of green-skinned Orions walked past. Geordi hadn't seen many Orions before, because they were neutral, not part of the Federation. He was surprised at how tall and muscular they were, even the women. He had heard that Pacifica was a favorite vacation spot for Orions.

The tallest of the Orions stopped to look at him. "Is that a Coridan phase modulator?" he asked.

"Yes, it is," said Geordi.

"Would you like to sell it?"

"I'm afraid I can't."

The Orion looked at the others in the group, who had stopped to wait for him. "Go on," he said. They obeyed him and continued on their way.

He held out a green hand to Geordi. "Permit me to introduce myself. I am Jaktu."

"Geordi La Forge," said the cadet. He stood and shook the man's hand. The Orion's grip was extremely strong.

"Now that we know each other, will you reconsider?"

"I'm sorry," said Geordi, "it's not mine to sell. Besides, it's not working."

"Pity," said the Orion with a smile. "Those things

can be tricky. Try reversing the polarity of the attenuators."

"Really?" Geordi answered. "I'll try that. Thanks."

"You're with the Starfleet Academy Band, aren't you?"

"Yes," said Geordi proudly.

Jaktu nodded. "I'm one of the judges. I'm looking forward to hearing your band. I've heard that your music is very inspirational."

"Well, thank you," said Geordi. "I hope you like us."

"I'm sure I will. I'll see you in the concert hall." The Orion smiled pleasantly and went to catch up with his group.

Hmmm, thought Geordi. He had always heard that Orions were brutish and warlike. Jaktu seemed quite the gentleman. The cadet took some small tools out of his bag and opened the phase modulator. He disconnected two wires, reversed them, and closed the case.

Not expecting much, he turned on the instrument and pressed a few keys. A loud train whistle sounded, and several people on the bridge turned to look at him.

"All right!" said Geordi with relief. Now he had time to find their room, get something to eat, then hit the beach!

It was 1855 hours, and Geordi was pacing backstage at Titan Hall. He cradled the phase modulator to his chest. Now that he had gotten it working, he wasn't going to let it out of his sight. But that wasn't what was making him nervous.

What made him nervous was that Will Riker was nowhere to be seen.

A group of Saurian singers were onstage. To human ears, they sounded more like a pack of alley cats in a fight, but the audience applauded warmly. In a few minutes, the Starfleet Academy Band was going on!

Stinson walked past him, blowing muffled notes on his trumpet. "Hey, where's the bathing-suit boy?"

"He'll be here," Geordi answered, hoping that was true.

Geordi turned to look at Will's music stand and trombone, which were right where they were supposed to be. The only thing missing was Will. Captain Webb and Commander Baxter were running over the music charts, and they hadn't yet noticed he was missing.

Then Geordi remembered the communicator badge on his chest. That was why he was wearing it, for emergencies like this. He rushed off to a quiet corner and tapped his badge.

"La Forge to Riker," he said. "Come in, Will Riker!"

A relaxed voice came on. "Oh, hi, Geordi. What's up?"

"What's up?" yelled Geordi. Akusta walked by and gave him a funny look, and he lowered his voice. "We're onstage in two minutes. Where are you?"

"Oh, no!" came a shocked voice. "I'm still on the beach, in my bathing suit!"

"Will!" shouted Geordi. "You've got to get over here!"

"But I don't have my uniform!" Will paused. "Listen,

Stinson is smaller than me, but I could wear *his* uniform, and he could wear *yours.*"

"Okay," muttered Geordi. "Just get here as quickly as you can! La Forge out."

Geordi ran over to Stinson and dragged the trumpet player into the corner. "Take your uniform off."

"What are you talking about?" asked Stinson.

"Riker is coming in late, and he's still in his bathing suit! He's too big to wear my uniform, but he could wear yours, and you could wear mine."

Stinson growled. "That goof-off. I'll strangle him!" Still, he started to take off his uniform.

Onstage, the announcer said, "Let's have a big round of applause for the Saurian Seminary Singers." The applause made Geordi and Stinson remove their clothes even faster.

A few seconds later, Stinson was wearing a uniform several sizes too small. And Geordi was crouched behind a bank of speakers—in his T-shirt and underwear. He was holding Stinson's uniform in front of him.

"I'm going to kill that guy," grumbled Stinson.

"I'll help you," said Geordi.

Commander Baxter walked by and shouted, "Take your places!" Then she stopped and turned slowly to look at the cadets in the dark corner. Geordi crouched down even further and pretended to fiddle with the phase modulator.

"Mr. Stinson," said Baxter, "isn't your uniform a bit small for you?"

"Yes," he breathed, almost popping a button. "It's all Riker's fault! If he wasn't late—"

"He's not late," snapped Baxter. "He's right over there. In fact, he's been out front, watching the show. Now quit goofing around, and take your places."

Stinson and Geordi turned to see Will Riker step out from behind a curtain. He was wearing his uniform and grinning from ear to ear. As he walked past them, he said to Stinson, "That's for the broken chair."

"What did I do to you?" asked Geordi.

"You didn't trust me," said Will. "I do like to have fun, but I know the difference between fun and duty. If I say I'll be somewhere, I'll be there."

Stinson was sputtering and turning red with anger. "Riker, let me tell you—"

The announcer interrupted him. "Direct from Earth, we are pleased to present the Starfleet Academy Band!"

As the audience applauded, Geordi rushed off to a corner and began to pull on the pants that were too big. Stinson ran to his seat, but when he sat down his pants ripped. There were chuckles all around.

The laughter relaxed the young musicians, and they opened the concert with a rousing rendition of "Minnie the Moocher." That night, Starfleet Academy Band gave its best concert of the year. At least that was Geordi's opinion, and he had heard all their concerts and rehearsals.

During "Take the A Train," Geordi waited tensely with his fingers on the Coridan phase modulator. His pants started to fall down, but still he kept his fingers on the keys. At the exact moment, he tapped the keys and blew the train whistle.

Wooo-wooo! It sounded great.

Then came the closing number, "Stardust," and Geordi had never heard them play it better. Stinson had the honor of playing the solo, and he had to stand up in his ripped pants. Luckily his back was facing away from the audience.

When they were done, the applause was loud and long. Everybody in the band grinned at each other. They knew they had blown them away! Captain Webb just kept nodding over and over again, and Commander Baxter jabbed her fist into the air.

Geordi thought the applause would never stop, but it finally did. The curtain came down, and the band members hugged each other and shook hands. The announcer said there would be an intermission, and the houselights came on.

Commander Baxter clapped her hands. "Pack up your instruments! There are other groups coming on after us."

"Excellent job!" declared Captain Webb. "If we're not finalists, there is no justice in the universe."

"I think you will be finalists," said a deep voice.

Geordi turned around to see the tall Orion, Jaktu, striding onto the stage. He waved to Geordi. "Mr. La Forge, perhaps you would introduce me to your director."

Holding his pants up, Geordi rushed out to greet the green-skinned alien. He escorted him to the captain. "Captain Webb," he said, "this is Jaktu. He's one of the judges."

The Orion took Webb's hand and pumped it fiercely. "That was wonderful! You are even better than I had heard you were. One would think you were professional musicians."

"Why, thank you," said Captain Webb with a big grin. "Do you really think we'll make the finals?"

"You will, if I have anything to say about it." Jaktu lowered his voice. "In fact, you are so good that I must have you play at one of our outposts. I can offer you good payment and a grateful audience. My ship is in orbit, and we can leave right after the competition is over."

"That is very flattering," said Webb, "but they aren't professional musicians. They're all Starfleet cadets, and they have to get back to the Academy."

Jaktu frowned as if he hadn't expected to be turned down. "When can you play for me?"

The captain shrugged. "All of our engagements must be approved by the Academy. You would have to make arrangements with our superintendent's office."

The Orion's dark eyes narrowed. "I see. There is always so much red tape, isn't there? I will have to see if I can cut through the red tape. My congratulations to you, Captain. I look forward to hearing you again tomorrow, and perhaps soon after that." He bowed and walked away.

The captain smiled at Geordi. "Well, we have at least one fan. Good job, La Forge, on the modulator."

"Thank you, sir."

"Keep it with you. I may want to work it into more numbers."

"Yes, sir!" said Geordi with a grin. Now he really felt like part of the band.

CHAPTER

5

As Jaktu had promised, the Starfleet Academy Band was one of three finalists invited to return the next night. But before that concert there were twenty-two hours of daylight in which to have fun, and Geordi and Will decided to make the most of it.

After breakfast, Geordi took Will in search of a forcefield roller coaster. They finally found one at the end of a shiny metal pier. It didn't look like much, just a line of small, colorful boats parked in the water. A sign said they'd be open in five minutes.

"All right!" exclaimed Geordi. "We'll be the first ones on."

Will looked at him puzzledly. "On what? They're just little boats."

"That's what they look like," said Geordi, "but there's more to it than that. You'll see."

Will grinned. "Scary, huh?"

"It will curl your hair."

"How many cadets know about this?"

Geordi shrugged. "I think I'm the only one in the band who's ever been to Pacifica before. Want to try it?"

"Wait a minute." Will tapped his communicator badge. "Riker to Akusta."

"Hello, Will," said the Deltan female. "What are you doing today?"

Will gave his friend a wink. "Geordi and I are about to take a boat ride. Want to come along?"

"Sure!"

"Better hurry. There's a silver pier at the end of the Strand. Do you know where that is?"

"Sure, I can see it from here."

"Then hurry. Riker out."

Geordi looked at him and shook his head. "You sure hold a grudge, don't you?"

"They started it," said Riker. "Once I get even with Akusta, I can quit the band with a clear conscience."

Geordi frowned. "Are you still thinking about quitting the band? Why?"

"They're never going to give me a break here. They would rather have Leshelle, even though he's gone."

"Give them a chance," said Geordi. "They're just getting to know you. Being in the band is not about playing music—it's about teamwork. That's what everything in the Academy is about."

"Then why do they pick on me?" muttered Will. He looked off into the distance. "Here she comes. Don't say anything."

Geordi shrugged. "I never say anything."

He turned to see the tall Deltan striding toward them. She was wearing her bathing suit, which was good, Geordi thought, because she was going to get wet. At least the roller coaster was not going to curl Akusta's hair, because she didn't have any.

Will waved to her. "Hurry up!"

When Akusta reached them, she looked doubtfully at the little boats. "This looks boring."

"Oh, it will be fun," insisted Will. "Come on."

As they walked out on the pier, a flock of colorful birds flew overhead. A dozen flying fish leapt out of the water, and the birds turned in formation to chase them. *Pacifica is a beautiful place,* thought Geordi, and he would be sad to leave after the concert.

At the end of the pier, a Tiburion with huge ears was polishing one of the boats.

"Are you open yet?" asked Riker.

The Tiburion checked his timepiece. "Yes, I sure am."

"How much does it cost?" asked Akusta.

"Your money's not good here," answered the man. "I saw your band perform last night. You were wonderful."

The three of them grinned. "Thank you," answered Akusta. "We'll be performing again tonight."

"I wouldn't miss it," said the man. "Do you know what to expect from this ride?"

"Sure we do," Will answered quickly. "Can we all fit into one boat?"

The proprietor pointed to the first boat in line, a sleek red craft. "Hop in."

Will smiled at Akusta. "You sit in front."

They all squeezed into the tiny boat, with Akusta and Will in front, followed by Geordi. Geordi had an attack of guilt, and he almost warned the Deltan that they were going on a wild ride. But when Akusta and Stinson were out to get Will, he hadn't warned him. It was only fair to keep quiet now.

The Tiburion gave them a sly grin. "Have fun." He picked up a small control panel.

Akusta still looked bored. "I hope this doesn't take too long."

"Don't worry about that," said Geordi. "It'll be over quickly."

A second later they took off like a shot, rising straight into the air on invisible forcefields. Akusta started screaming in terror, and she never stopped for the whole crazy ride.

When they got about thirty meters into the air, the tiny craft plummeted back toward the water. Now all three of them were yelling! Akusta covered her eyes as they leveled out and streaked across the water, shooting a stream of water high into the air.

Then they shot into the air again and swerved around on an invisible track. All three of them were thrown to one side of the boat, and Akusta wailed in fear.

"Stop this thing! Stop it!"

But it was too late for that. They barely had time to catch a breath as the craft plunged again toward the waves. This time the boat sunk deeper into the water, and the spray drenched the three riders.

Akusta huddled with fear and screamed, "We're out of control!"

Riker roared with laughter. "Fun, isn't it?"

The Deltan looked at him as if he were crazy. The craft jumped out of the water and bounced up and down rapidly many times as it flew across the water. Geordi felt as if he had left his stomach back on the pier.

All three of them were pale and soaking wet by the time the craft spun around and bounced to a stop at the pier. The Tiburion was grinning at them.

"Want to go again?" he asked.

"No!" shouted Akusta. She tried to stand up but was too dizzy. She nearly fell out of the boat, and Will had to catch her.

"You weren't bored, were you?" he asked.

Her dark eyes tore into him. "I never want to see *you* again, either." Somehow she crawled out of the craft and staggered down the pier.

Will gave Geordi a satisfied smile. "What is it that the Klingons say? 'Revenge is a dish best served cold.' "

"Cold and wet," added Geordi, shaking the water out of his VISOR.

That night at the performance, Akusta's eyes were still shooting daggers at Will. Geordi feared that she and Stinson would try to get their own revenge, but he doubted they would try tonight. The band had a chance to go home winners, and nobody was going to mess that up.

There was another reason to be serious. The Starfleet Academy Band was playing last, and they had already heard the other two groups who were finalists. They were really good.

The Merakan Youth Symphony played amazing arrangements with syncopated rhythms. Maybe their music didn't have the melodies of Earth jazz, but the Merakans were fine musicians. In their culture almost everyone played an instrument, and these players were the best of the best.

The other group was from Delthara University on Alpha Centauri VII. A very practical people, the Centaurians played instruments made from household objects. Geordi watched in awe as they coaxed music from vacuum cleaners, inner tubes, and pots and pans.

It had been easier the night before, when the Academy Band had been one of the first groups to perform. Nobody had known what to expect. Now with everyone watching they played well, but not as well as the night before. They were nervous, and it showed.

Maybe, thought Geordi, they would be more relaxed if they had someone rip his pants every night, as Stinson had done. Even Geordi was nervous. During "Take the A Train," he missed sounding the train whistle by half a beat.

On "Stardust," Burt Hosteen played the solo on his saxophone, and he simply wasn't as good as Stinson and some of the other soloists. The Starfleet Academy

43

Band finished second to the Merakans, but nobody complained. The Merakans had clearly deserved to win.

Captain Webb was very gracious when he accepted the award for second place. He got a lot of applause when he promised the audience that the Starfleet Academy Band would be back next year.

Geordi was seated at the rear of the concert hall, and he was surprised when Jaktu sat down beside him.

"This is a travesty," said the Orion. "I put you in first place, but the other judges overruled me."

"We weren't as good as last night," Geordi said sadly. "It happens."

The Orion's green face wrinkled into a frown. "It happened because your director allowed you too much time for amusement. If you had rehearsed all day, you would have been better. I am a strong believer in discipline."

"Well," said Geordi, "we're only students. If we don't have any fun, what's the point in coming here?"

The Orion narrowed his dark eyes at Geordi. "The point is to *win*. That is always the point."

Geordi wasn't going to argue with him. He wasn't sure that he really liked Jaktu all that much.

"Are you leaving tonight?" asked the Orion.

"As soon as this is over," said Geordi.

"Very well." Jaktu stood and offered his strong hand to Geordi. "We will meet again."

"I hope so," said Geordi, trying to be polite. At least the Orion was a big fan of theirs, so he couldn't be all bad. The cadet sat back in his seat and watched the end of the awards ceremony.

* * *

An hour later, the cadets transported back to the *Gallant* and got their duty assignments. Geordi and Will were both surprised to find that they were assigned to the bridge. They were supposed to report immediately.

"All right!" said Will excitedly. "Bridge duty—this is more like it!"

"But I wanted Engineering," grumbled Geordi.

Will patted him on the back. "The bridge is the place to be. That's where the action is. I don't intend to serve anywhere else."

"I guess it's better than the mess hall," said Geordi.

They reported to the small bridge of the *Gallant* and found Lieutenant Commander Baxter in command. She motioned them to the auxilary consoles in the aft command area.

"Mr. Riker," she said, "monitor operations. Mr. La Forge, monitor life-support. Don't enter any commands unless I give you a direct order."

"Yes, sir!" said Riker smartly. "Commander, we sincerely appreciate this assignment."

She gave them a slight smile. "You two came through for us in a big way, and you deserve a reward. If there's an emergency, be ready to relieve the command crew. But I don't think we'll have an emergency."

"Me neither," answered Will confidently.

He and Geordi took their stations on the aft consoles and watched Baxter and the regular crew prepare to leave orbit. It was exciting being on the bridge, Geordi had to admit. Maybe he would try for a bridge assignment when he graduated. He had been doing well in his navigation classes.

After running through the predeparture checklist, Baxter ordered, "Helm, take us out of orbit at one-third impulse."

"Yes, sir," came the response.

As ordered, Geordi monitored the ship's life-support systems. Even though the *Gallant* was an old training cruiser, she was well maintained. He detected only a few minor power fluctuations when the impulse engines went on-line.

"Distance from the planet?" asked Baxter.

"Twenty thousand kilometers," answered the operations officer.

Baxter nodded. "Helm, set course for Earth, maximum warp."

"Yes, sir," answered the helmsman. "Course laid in."

"Engage," ordered Baxter.

"Engaging warp," said the ensign.

Suddenly the ship was rocked by a powerful concussion, and Geordi was nearly thrown out of his seat.

"Report!" demanded Baxter.

The officer on Ops stared at his console, and his eyes grew as large as the twin suns of Pacifica. "Commander, that was phaser fire. We are under attack!"

"Shields up! Red alert!" shouted Baxter. The dark-haired woman stalked across the bridge. "Communications, advise Starfleet."

The ensign on the comm panel shook her head in amazement. "Captain, a dampening field is suppressing our communications!"

"Commander!" shouted the ensign on the weapons

console. "Shields aren't responding. They've been disabled by the dampening field *and* a tractor beam!"

"A tractor beam?" The commander stared at the blank viewscreen overhead. "From where? Short-range scanners, report."

"I have found the source of the tractor beam," said the Ops officer.

"On screen."

A large warship filled the main viewer. It was green and black and shaped like a torpedo with fins. The sleek craft bore down on the small cruiser like a shark attacking a sea lion.

"They're Orion," said Baxter with amazement. "Arm photon torpedoes!"

The ship was jolted again by phaser fire, and the Ops console exploded in a flash of sparks and flame. The wounded ensign fell to the floor, and Will dashed to the console and dragged him to safety. Geordi grabbed a fire extinguisher off the bulkhead and sprayed the console until the flames sputtered out.

Baxter slapped the panel on the command chair. "Sickbay, medteam to the bridge."

"Commander!" called the communications officer. "I have just received a message from the Orion vessel."

"Yes?"

The young officer swallowed hard. "They say—if we resist, we will be destroyed."

CHAPTER

6

Geordi heard a *whoosh,* and he turned to see the turbolift door open. Three members of the medteam ran onto the bridge and took charge of the wounded ensign. Captain Webb followed them and approached Baxter.

"Report?" he demanded.

Baxter looked grimly at her comrade. "We've been attacked by an Orion warship, and they've locked on with a tractor beam. A dampening field has cut off our communications as well as our shields. If we resist, they say they'll destroy us."

Captain Webb stared at the torpedolike vessel on the viewscreen. "What on Earth could they want with *us?"*

Suddenly the *Gallant* was jolted again, and everyone staggered to stay on their feet.

"Sir, they've locked on to us with a tractor beam," said the helmsman. "We are moving."

"Moving where?" demanded Webb. "Hail that vessel."

"I'm sorry, sir," said the comm officer. "The dampening field won't allow us to communicate out."

"We could defend ourselves," said Baxter. "But I don't think we can slug it out with an Orion warship."

Captain Webb looked around at his young crew, plus the two cadets, Geordi and Will. From his concerned expression, Geordi could almost read his mind. His anger told him to fight back, but his experience told him to wait. The deaths of all of the young people aboard the *Gallant* weren't worth a show of force.

The viewscreen went blank, and the lights dimmed on the bridge.

"We have entered warp drive," said the helmsman. "Their tractor beam is holding steady."

"Any idea of our destination?" asked Webb.

The officer shook his head. "I've plotted a vector of our course, and it's *not* the Orion homeworld. We are now at warp two and increasing speed."

Baxter frowned. "This old ship can't go much faster than warp two without falling apart."

Geordi glanced at Will, and he could see the fear in his friend's eyes. Thus far, only the people on the bridge knew what was happening. As Will had said, the bridge was where the action was. Serving on the bridge also meant that you were the first to know that the ship was in trouble.

"Ready photon torpedoes," ordered Webb. "We may have to use them if they try to take us much faster."

"Our speed is holding steady at warp three," said the helmsman with relief.

Geordi went back to his station and studied his life-support readouts. There were power fluctuations all over the ship, but nothing serious. At least they weren't going to die by being dragged somewhere at warp speed.

Will took his place at the auxilary Ops station. With the regular Ops station out, he was on duty. He reported, "Tractor beam steady at warp three-point-two."

"This is crazy," said Captain Webb. "Why would the Orions hijack an old training vessel full of Starfleet cadets?"

Geordi snapped his fingers. "Jaktu."

"Jaktu?" asked Webb.

The cadet nodded. "Remember, sir, the Orion judge. He wanted us to play for him on some outpost. He didn't like it when you told him no. He said he would cut through the red tape."

The rotund captain nodded. "I remember. It's great to have fans, but this is ridiculous."

Webb strode to the captain's chair and tapped the comm panel. "This is Captain Webb to all hands. Our ship is in a tractor beam, and we are being hijacked to an unknown destination. Our hijackers are Orion, and we *think* they are hijacking us to play music somewhere."

The captain shook his head at the madness of it. "At any rate, we must remain calm. We have not offered any resistance, but we will if our lives are endangered.

We are standing down from red to yellow alert. All hands, remain at your posts. Webb out."

He looked at Geordi. "You have a friendship with this Orion, right?"

"I wouldn't call it a friendship, but we did talk a few times."

"Then you are to stay on the bridge until further notice," said Webb. He looked around at his young crew. "There is nothing we can do now but wait."

For ten hours, they waited with no further word from their captors. A relief bridge crew came on duty, and everyone was relieved except for Geordi, Will Riker, and Captain Webb. The portly captain paced nervously across the narrow bridge of the *Gallant*.

Finally the helmsman reported. "We are coming out of warp drive. Our location is the Zyrapul solar system, in neutral space."

Captain Webb scratched his chin. "Zyrapul? What is the closest Federation planet?"

"Tellar, eight light-years away."

"That's not close enough to offer much help," said Webb. "Communications, can you send a message to Starfleet?"

"Negative, sir," answered the woman on communications. "The Orion dampening fields are still jamming us."

"Helm," said the captain, "stand by, in case we get a chance to break out of the tractor beam."

"Yes, sir."

"Sir!" shouted Cadet Riker. "Incoming transporter beam!"

Before anyone could react, six armed Orions materialized on the bridge. One of them was Jaktu. The weapons officer drew his phaser, and Geordi tensed, expecting a battle.

"Hold your fire," ordered Captain Webb. "Stand down."

"A wise decision," said Jaktu pleasantly. He nodded to his green-skinned officers and they lowered their weapons a few centimeters.

"What is the meaning of this?" demanded Captain Webb. "You can't hijack a Starfleet vessel! You may not be members of the Federation, but you have treaties with us. This is a serious breach of those treaties."

"You will be free to leave in a few hours," said Jaktu. He looked at Geordi and smiled. "I told you we would meet again. I'm glad to see you."

Geordi rose to his feet. "I'm not glad to see *you,* not like this."

The Orion shrugged. "I couldn't get your wonderful band to play for me any other way, and I desperately need you. Before you decide that I'm an evil person, may I have a moment to explain?"

Captain Webb glanced at Geordi. Outnumbered, outgunned, and far away from Federation space, they didn't seem to have much choice.

"Proceed," said Webb through clenched teeth.

The Orion motioned to the overhead viewscreen. "Can you find the fourth planet in this solar system?"

Webb nodded to Will on the auxiliary console. A few seconds later, a dark green planet with large landmasses appeared on the screen. They could see flashes of light

on the planet's surface, and dense clouds of black
smoke hung in the air.

The Orion pointed to the dark planet. "This planet,
Elofim, is disputed territory. We have thirty thousand
troops fighting a terrible war on the planet's surface.
They have been fighting for three years without relief,
without leave."

He looked at Geordi. "These soldiers are no older than
most of you, and they are away from home for the first
time in their lives. The war is brutal, and their morale is
low. They need some entertainment, some inspiration.
They need to see the Starfleet Academy Band!"

"What?"

Jaktu held his hands out to Captain Webb. "I beg
you, sir, please come down and give one performance.
It would mean so much to these young soldiers. The
enemy is going through a period of resupply, and the
hostilities have lessened for a brief time. That is why it
was so urgent that I bring you here now.

"For one hour," begged the Orion, "let them forget
there is a war. Let them forget that death is in the air—
let them hear music instead. Is that too much to ask?"

Captain Webb's expression softened a little. "Don't the
Orions have any bands that could play at the battlefront?"

Jaktu shook his head. "Orions are not known for
their musical ability. We have dancing girls, but that
would not be appropriate. Your band is perfect—they
are entertaining and inspirational. Especially that ragtime number."

"If I refuse?" asked Webb.

Jaktu licked his purple lips and stroked his green brow.

"Please don't, Captain Webb. I asked you nicely once, and you refused. So you forced me to bring you here. If you refuse again, I don't know what you will force me to do."

Captain Webb frowned, obviously not happy with his choices. "Can you guarantee our safety?"

The Orion nodded. "Yes. Not only will you be surrounded by thirty thousand troops, but we will be in orbit to beam you up. I promise, you will be free to leave right after your concert. This will be the largest, most grateful audience you have ever faced. I'm begging you, Captain."

Captain Webb looked at Geordi, and the young cadet wondered what he would decide. Certainly it was a noble aim to entertain troops at the front. In the long history of the Starfleet Academy Band, they had done so many times.

The captain sighed. "I haven't got much choice, but I want you to come with us. And I suggest you go through proper channels next time."

The Orion grinned. "You won't regret this, Captain, once you see their faces." He lifted his communicator and spoke into the device. "Beam back everyone but me. Then set course for Elofim. Tell them that we will have our glorious concert after all!"

Half an hour later, the band members stood waiting in line outside the transporter room of the *Gallant*. They were wearing their dress uniforms and holding their instruments. Geordi gripped the Coridan phase modulator in his hands, and Will Riker had his trombone.

Stinson and Akusta edged up to them. "You were on the bridge," said Stinson. "What's going on?"

Will pointed at Geordi. "La Forge has got an Orion friend who wants us to play a concert for him."

Geordi scowled. "He's *not* my friend. But I can tell you why we were brought here. There are thirty thousand Orion troops on Elofim, and we're supposed to play and cheer them up."

"So they can fight and die cheerfully," added Will.

Akusta scowled. "If this is another practical joke, I'm going to break you in half."

"It's no joke," said Will.

When they wound their way into the transporter room, they found Captain Webb and Jaktu checking off the young musicians.

"Thank you," said Jaktu to each cadet. "Orion will never forget you."

"Yes," said Will, "but will you help me take my propulsion exam? I'm missing my class right now."

"I will send my thanks to your superiors," promised the Orion.

Geordi and Will took their places on the transporter platform, and Will whispered, "Do you know what to expect down there?"

"A war zone," Geordi guessed. He wondered how bad it would be.

"Energize," ordered Captain Webb.

Geordi took a deep breath and hugged the phase modulator to his chest. Normally he didn't mind transporting, but this time fear gnawed his stomach.

CHAPTER

7

Geordi felt a cool wind on his face. It would have been refreshing except for the foul stench that came with it. The smell was a combination of burning debris, spilled fuel, sweat, and death.

He stared through his VISOR to discover an amazing sight—Elofim was not an uninhabited planet as he had imagined. There were skyscrapers and modern buildings, only now they were empty, bombed-out ruins. Whole walls had tumbled down, and smoke curled from blackened windows.

Scattered about were a few delicate spires, statues, and stained-glass windows, proving that Elofim must have been a beautiful place at one time. Now it was a wasteland of broken concrete, smashed glass, and green-skinned Orions.

There had to be at least a hundred Orion soldiers guarding the field where they had beamed down. *It must look odd,* thought Geordi—an army of grubby, battle-weary soldiers meeting a band of young people in sparkling dress uniforms.

Getting curious, the soldiers edged closer, and the young cadets backed up. They gripped their musical instruments as if they might be stolen by this grungy crowd. The Orions returned the reaction and gripped their bazookalike phaser rifles as if they were more important.

Geordi saw both men and women among the green-skinned soldiers. With their sunken faces and blank eyes, they looked as burned out as the buildings.

"Attention!" shouted a grizzled old Orion. The soldiers fell into a rough line and shouldered their weapons.

"That's better," said the Old Orion, who seemed to be a sergeant. "These people have come a long way to entertain you. They want to show you that you have not been forgotten."

That's not exactly true, thought Geordi. The cadets didn't want to be here either, but now was not the time to mention that. They were going to leave after the concert, but these young soldiers were going to stay behind. Many of them would probably die on this forgotten planet.

"Escort them to the amphitheater," ordered the sergeant.

One young soldier stepped up to Geordi. "This way, please." He walked off, and Geordi fell into step beside him.

"Have you been here long?" asked Geordi.

The Orion looked around nervously, as if it was forbidden to talk. No one seemed to be paying attention to them. "Three years," he said softly.

"This must be an important planet for you to fight so hard," said Geordi.

The Orion looked down. "We are mercenaries. We are fighting because it is our job."

Geordi tried not to look shocked. They weren't even fighting for their homeworld! They were doing this horrible work for some third party. He reminded himself that the Orions had only recently given up slavery. Most of them were from a poor working class who were used to selling themselves to survive.

They walked down a cluttered street and turned a corner. Geordi gasped. The "amphitheater" was nothing more than a huge crater with cement stubble for seats. In the center of the crater was a raised wooden stage, and it was surrounded by a sea of wary green faces.

It was hard to tell if there were ten, twenty, or thirty thousand of them seated in the rubble, but there were a lot. A murmur surged from the crowd, as if the entrance of the Starfleet Academy Band was some sort of miracle.

On the stage, Orions were setting up the band's music stands. Captain Webb, Commander Baxter, and Jaktu were present, overseeing the preparations.

Geordi noticed that his fellow roadies were not included in the group. He was the only nonmusician who had beamed down. Captain Webb probably didn't want to endanger any more people than he had to. Plus, Geordi knew Jaktu, and he was getting the hang of the Coridan phase modulator.

Will Riker stepped up behind him and gazed at the grim audience. "They look like the walking dead," he whispered. "This place is the pits. We shouldn't be playing here—we should be trying to *end* this stupid war."

"We can't interfere," said Geordi, "because the Orions don't belong to the Federation. All we can do is make these people forget their troubles for an hour or so."

Will headed up the stairs to the stage. "I know all about the Prime Directive, but this is crazy. Who is their enemy, anyway?"

Geordi shook his head. "Who knows? The Orions are only mercenaries fighting for money, and their enemy could be mercenaries, too. Who knows what parties are behind this conflict? Maybe it's a good thing that we stumbled upon it, so that we can report it to Starfleet."

"If we live long enough," muttered Will. He and Geordi strode onto the wooden stage and stared across the vast ocean of soldiers. The Orion soldiers were eerily quiet.

"Let's just play this gig and head home," said Will with a shiver.

Only it wasn't that simple. As the band began to play before the hushed throng, a strange thing happened.

The audience began to weep.

At first, it was disturbing to hear thousands of battle-weary Orions sobbing at their lively music. But the band began to realize that this raw show of emotion was a compliment.

That invisible thread between performers and audience is woven every performance, but that day it was especially strong. Every song they played connected hard with the weeping audience, especially the ragtime and blues numbers.

When Geordi hit the train whistle on "Take the A Train," the phase modulator howled like a lonely coyote. The band could do no wrong. They played every song they knew—some they had only rehearsed—and the concert ran over two hours.

When they finally ended with "Stardust," the clarinet player, Duperren, made his instrument wail. His lilting solo floated over the crowd, and a multitude of Orions wailed along with him. It sent chills all over Geordi's body, and his eyes welled with tears.

After "Stardust," they rose to take a bow, but there was no applause. Instead, the Orions jumped to their feet and roared at the top of their lungs! It was a ferocious shout, releasing all the pent-up rage at their terrible fate.

The band members were grinning like fools, basking in the glory. As Jaktu had said, they would never find an audience as grateful as this one.

As the musicians bowed and waved, Geordi noticed

something odd in the overcast sky. It was something a person without a VISOR might not see, because the mass of vapor trails were behind thick clouds.

Shuttlecraft were his first guess, but the trails were too small for shuttlecraft. They were more like one-man fighter aircraft. Strafing machines!

"Captain Webb!" shouted Geordi. He forced his way from the back of the stage through the chairs and band-stands of the musicians. Stinson grabbed Geordi with a beefy arm as he rushed past.

"Listen to that," said Stinson with a grin. "They love us!"

Geordi pointed into the sky. "Don't you see them?"

Stinson peered into the gloomy clouds and shook his head. "See what? Geordi, you need to sit down and relax."

With a swarm of deadly aircraft zooming down, Geordi had no choice but to ignore him. He waved like a madman and yelled, "Captain Webb! Captain Webb!"

The captain turned around at the same moment that a shrieking alarm ripped the air. The sound was so painful that Geordi dropped to his knees and gripped his ears. He tried to concentrate on what was happen-ing, but electromagnetic interference jolted his senses.

Someone had turned on some very powerful jamming equipment, and it reduced Geordi to a blind man. The Coridan phase modulator fell out of his hands, and he dropped to his knees to retrieve it. After all he had been through with that gizmo, he wasn't about to lose it!

Geordi groped around on the stage until he found

the oval-shaped device, then he hugged it to his chest. Alarmed shouts brought his attention back to the battle, and he looked up to find his vision returning.

The act of retrieving the phase modulator had helped clear his mind. Despite the sirens and jamming, Geordi found that he could control his VISOR if he concentrated.

He gazed upward to see a formation of sleek fighters punch through the clouds and come swooping toward the stage. Atop the stage, he was directly in their line of fire. Geordi held his breath, expecting to die.

Suddenly the first wave of ships went into weird tailspins, shooting harmlessly out of the way. Two of them crashed into each other, causing spectacular fireworks in the cloudy sky. Geordi gaped, and he wondered whether the electromagnetic interference was some sort of defensive weapon.

A second wave of ships came zooming in, and they apparently made an adjustment—they never wavered as they zoomed in for the kill.

Geordi looked over and saw many of his comrades from the band scurrying down the stairs. His momentary blindness had delayed him, but at least *they* were getting away! He turned back to the battle—to his horror, he found that he couldn't help watching.

The aircraft swooped down, firing narrow beams in a strafing pattern. Bravely the Orions leaped to their feet and returned fire with their bazooka-size phasers. Several aircraft erupted in flames, and the ground shuddered where they hit.

An explosion blasted out the right side of the stage

and Geordi was pitched off his feet. Clutching the phase modulator to his chest, he rolled off the slanted stage and fell into the dirt. Explosions erupted all around him, showering him with chunks of soil.

When Geordi tried to stand up, a large body plummeted into him and knocked him flat on his back. It was Will Riker! Will immediately began crawling back toward the stage, which was already in flames.

"Wait!" called Geordi. "We've got to beam up!" He banged the communicator badge on his chest, but nothing happened.

"Go ahead!" shouted Will. "You got my trombone working, and I'm not going to leave it behind. I'll be right back!"

Will hoisted himself back onto the creaking stage and crawled under the smoke and out of sight. Geordi slumped onto his back and watched the battle rage around them. He had seen space battles, but they were calm compared with a ground war. This was insanity—bedlam!

After a moment, he tried his commbadge again. There was no response. Whatever was jamming his VISOR was also jamming communications and the aircraft. With every passing second, more aircraft adjusted to the jamming. They broke through the clouds and swooped down on the stalwart Orion soldiers.

Geordi glanced around, looking for his comrades from the band, but they had scattered in all directions. This was pure survival—every man for himself. With no weapons or communications, the only option was to run.

But Geordi wasn't running. He was waiting for that stupid Riker to come back with his trombone!

Suddenly he heard a crunching sound, and the stage buckled further. He stared up to see a thin figure sailing through the air. Geordi barely managed to roll out of the way before Will fell on top of him.

Will grinned and held up his trombone. "Got it!"

The burning stage groaned loudly and tilted toward them. The cadets scurried out of the way as it collapsed with a *whoosh,* shooting a wall of sparks into the air. Geordi fell to the ground, coughing from the smoke and dust.

He felt a strong hand grab the back of his neck and propel him forward. "Come on!" shouted Will. "No time to rest!"

With a trombone in one hand and Geordi in the other, Will pounded up the hill. Geordi tripped and sprawled on top of something, and he opened his eyes to discover that it was a wounded Orion. When he looked closer, he gasped.

It was Jaktu! His green forehead had a scarlet gash across it, and he looked more dead than alive. The former music judge opened his eyes and stared at Geordi, then his bloody hand reached up and grabbed the cadet's dress uniform. The young cadet tried to pull away—but even dying, the Orion's grip was strong.

"I told you it was important you come," he said hoarsely. "Thank you . . . I am sorry for this. . . ."

"We've got to get you help!" shouted Geordi. Again he hit his commbadge, and again nothing happened.

The battle continued to rage all around, and nobody seemed to care that a man was dying.

"Too late," rasped Jaktu. "But I die with your music in my heart. I couldn't ask for a finer memory. . . ." He closed his eyes, and his hand slid away from Geordi's soiled dress uniform.

"Come on!" growled Will. "You can't help him now." Will dragged Geordi to his feet, and they crawled uphill together, trying to get out of the deadly crater.

An aircraft in flames screamed overhead and slammed into a building. The explosion knocked the cadets to the ground, and Geordi's mouth filled with dirt. The alarms wailed like banshees, and he couldn't see more than a meter through the thick smoke. Then he knew the truth. . . .

They were going to die out here, like Jaktu and the young soldiers. They had nothing to do with this war, but they were going to die just the same.

CHAPTER

8

As the battle howled around him, Geordi rose to his feet and dusted himself off. He spit out the dirt and wiped the back of his hand across his mouth. Then he picked up his phase modulator and made sure it was okay. Geordi had decided that if he was going to die on some weird planet, it would be on his feet, not cowering in fear.

"Will?" he shouted.

"Here!" called his friend. With his trombone leading the way, Will staggered out of the smoke. "Let's stick together."

"Right," agreed Geordi. "We've got to get underground, to a basement or a shelter."

With new resolve, the two of them climbed out of the crater. Where beautiful music had played only a few minutes ago, sirens, explosions, and jamming signals pounded Geordi's senses. But he discovered that by concentrating and keeping his fear in check, he could control his VISOR.

When they reached the lip of the crater, Geordi glanced back to get an overall picture. It wasn't a pretty sight. There were many fallen Orions, and the medics couldn't get to all of them. Enemy craft lay in burning hulks on the streets or sticking out of buildings at odd angles. Nobody rushed to help the enemy wounded.

Geordi shook his head at the futility of it. Their beautiful concert had turned into a disaster. The enemy must have known that thousands of Orions would be gathered in one place. They struck when they could create the maximum number of casualties. It was just one more element of insanity in the chaos.

There came a sudden lull in the noise level. Orion soldiers started regrouping and falling back. A few aircraft kept streaking across the sky, but most of them were massing in formation behind the clouds. Geordi doubted whether anyone could see the craft but him. Were they massing for another attack?

Will Riker frowned at a new dent on his trombone. "When you join Starfleet Academy Band, they never tell you that people will be trying to *kill* you."

Geordi grabbed Riker's arm and dragged him toward the nearest buildings. "Come on, we've got to get to cover."

"Wait a minute," said Will. "It got quieter. Is the battle over?"

"No," snapped Geordi. His acute hearing already picked up the whine of dozens of aircraft homing in. The sirens never stopped wailing, and he could sense the jamming frequencies shifting again. This battle wasn't over by a long shot.

The sensory input continued to flow into Geordi's head, but he could process it now. He got the feeling that this was a decisive battle, made critical by the presence of outsiders. If the band escaped and returned home, this war would cease to be a dirty little secret.

The Orions sensed it, too, as they trained their weapons on the sky. They looked as if they were ready to fight until the end.

The whine of jet engines buzzed in his skull, and Geordi knew that they had to seek underground shelter. He didn't think any place on the planet's surface would really be safe, but the ground offered the thickest protection.

He spotted stairs going down into an alley. It was a long city block to the alley, so he punched Will in the shoulder to get him moving. "Come on!"

"Hey, that hurt!"

Geordi began to run. "Those aircraft will hurt a lot more, and they're coming back!"

Will glanced over his shoulder. No aircraft were in sight yet, but he didn't need much encouragement to run for it. He hefted his trombone and jogged into a street that was littered with bricks, glass, and wreckage.

Before they had gotten halfway down the block they

heard shouts, followed by thunderous explosions. Geordi whirled around to see a sleek aircraft floating over the street. It raked the sidewalks and storefronts with deadly beams.

Geordi and Will skidded around a corner and charged into the alleyway, just as a beam shattered the sidewalk where they had been. The craft veered off but it banked slowly, as if coming back to look for them.

Without thinking, Geordi leapt over a railing and plunged down a narrow stairwell. He stumbled over the rubble, but he still managed to claw his way to the bottom. Will tumbled down after him, howling as he scraped against the wall.

The aircraft swept over the alley and cut loose with its beamed weapons. The building above them shuddered, and debris cascaded down. Geordi feared they would be crushed.

Beaten and bruised, Will hauled himself to his feet, reared back, and kicked the wooden door to pieces. What was left of the glass shattered everywhere. He smashed the frame off its hinges and dragged Geordi inside just as a block of cement thudded down the stairs.

It was dark and smelly inside the basement. The only light came from a small, broken window on street level. Water leaked from somewhere and formed a scummy pool in the corner. The basement was empty except for a few old rags, boxes, and spent hypos.

Geordi guessed that the place might have been used as a field hospital. Now it was too filthy for that or any other use.

Will picked up a small sign from the wreckage and shook his head. "Just our luck—it says this building has been condemned."

A resounding explosion shook the building to its foundation, and Geordi shrunk against the wall. He waited for the ceiling to collapse on top of them, but it held—somehow.

A second later, he heard the scream of a wounded aircraft streaking across the sky and plowing into a building. Geordi tapped his commbadge, not expecting any response. He wasn't disappointed.

"Communications still out," he muttered. "I wonder how the others are doing?"

"Maybe the *Gallant* was able to beam some of them aboard," said Will. He didn't sound as if he believed it.

"I hope there aren't ships fighting in orbit," said Geordi. "How do we know this war is just on the ground?"

Will shook his head and sat down. "We don't. We don't know anything, except that we're caught in the crossfire."

Outside, the explosions sounded farther away, as if the battle was moving on. *Or,* thought Geordi, *maybe we're just getting used to the horrible sounds.* He and Will didn't speak for several minutes, as they strained to hear anyone approaching.

Finally Will spoke. "Do you think serving in Starfleet is like this, with danger all the time?"

Geordi shook his head. "I grew up in Starfleet, and I don't remember it being like that. But maybe my parents didn't tell me when a situation was really bad.

There's danger in space, and hostile forces, but Starfleet *prevents* more problems than they get into.''

"If only we could get the warring parties to sit down and talk. What are they fighting for? There's nothing left of this stupid planet!'' Will pounded his fist on the dirty floor, and a cloud of dust whirled upward.

Geordi sighed. "Sometimes wars go on way beyond any kind of common sense. Maybe the parties got tired of fighting, so they hired Orions and other mercenaries. Now they keep the war going, without losing any of their own people.''

A box moved on the other side of the room, and Geordi and Will both jumped. Will staggered to his feet and stared nervously at the trash in the corner. "What was that?''

Geordi squinted at the box, not quite believing his VISOR. It moved again, and a small, furry animal dashed out, scurried across the floor, and disappeared under a clump of rags. It looked as if the creature was trying not to be caught.

"Yuck," said Will, wrinkling his nose. "Rats."

Geordi stared through his VISOR. "I'm not so sure it is a rat.''

"Well, maybe it's a mouse or a gopher, but it's in the rodent family.''

"Maybe.'' Geordi got on his hands and knees and began to crawl toward the old clump of rags, where the rodent had taken refuge.

Will frowned. "What are you doing, Geordi? Eventually we might get hungry enough to catch rats for food, but I'm not there yet.''

71

"Me neither," Geordi assured him. "You wouldn't want to eat this rat, anyway, because it's not alive."

"What do you mean, it's not alive? We just saw it *running.*"

Geordi shrugged as he edged closer to the rags. "You know how I see things differently than you do. I see things like thermal energy. All mammals give off heat, but not this one. Instead it gives off trace amounts of radiation."

Will frowned. "A radioactive rat? Come on, Geordi, don't go crazy on me."

"It's not a rat. Of course, it might be a creature that's very alien to us."

"Great," said Will. "That still doesn't explain why you want to catch it."

"Curiosity," answered Geordi. He reached out, grabbed the rags, and yanked them into the air. A furry animal with a silver tail squeaked and snarled at him. Then it lunged for his face!

Will's boot caught the critter just centimeters from Geordi's nose and sent it flying through the air. It bounced off a wall and fell into a pool of scum on the floor. Panting, Geordi turned to look at the rodent.

It squirmed on its back for a few seconds, and bright sparks arced into the water from its stomach. Then it rolled over and dashed toward a hole in the wall.

Will blinked in amazement. "Hey, did that rat just give off sparks?"

Geordi lunged to block the hole, and the rat skidded to a stop. Fearful it would bite him, Geordi yelled, "Get away! Go!"

The thing reversed course and headed toward Will.

"That's what I've been trying to tell you!" said Geordi. "It's a tiny robot disguised to *look* like a rodent. It's probably transmitting information. It may be a spy."

"A spy?" Will lifted his foot and stomped the rat as it scurried past.

He caught its tail under his heel, and the mechanical beast turned to snap at him with gleaming teeth. In reflex, Will jerked his foot back, and the rat escaped, leaving behind a few centimeters of its tail. To Geordi, the tail looked like an antenna.

Geordi grabbed one of the boxes off the floor and gave chase. "Get the rags!" he shouted. "Something to throw over it!"

Will dutifully grabbed a handful of grimy rags and joined the hunt. Geordi tried not to think of the absurdity of two guys crawling around in a basement trying to catch a mechanical rat, while a war raged all around them.

They finally herded the rat into a corner, and it had nowhere to run. With mechanical repetition, it snarled and snapped at them.

"If we catch it," asked Riker doubtfully, "what are we going to do with it?"

"It's a reconnaissance robot," said Geordi. "It may be communicating with those fighters up there. Maybe it told them about the gathering of Orions—maybe it could tell *us* how to get out of here. Or who's behind this war."

Will smiled wearily. "I thought you said that we couldn't do anything about the war."

"That's before I was in it," said Geordi. "A device like this must have some electronic signatures. Are you ready?"

"Yeah."

Geordi tossed his box over the mechanical rat, and Will flung his rags like a net. It worked, and they trapped the tiny robot under several layers of debris.

The creature banged around inside of the box and tried to gnaw its way out. Geordi plopped on top of the box and struggled to keep it down. He only hoped that the thing wouldn't gnaw its way through the top.

"Grab the modulator!" shouted Geordi. The box bounced up and down beneath him.

Will stared at him. "What?"

"Grab my phase modulator! We've got to shut this thing off. Maybe I can jam its circuits."

Will nodded and picked up the strange oval-shaped device from the floor. He handed it to Geordi, who turned it on and began to press buttons.

The phase modulator was actually a very sophisticated device capable of generating much more than sound waves. By phase shifting, it could affect brain waves and relax the listener, or so the Coridans claimed. At the very least, it could transmit an amazing array of frequencies.

In the close quarters of the basement, Geordi bombarded the little robot with waves. The phase modulator began to shriek, and Will held his hands over his ears. Geordi kept pressing buttons while the thing in the box kept bumping, fighting, and gnawing.

Finally the frequencies went beyond the range of human hearing, and Will slumped against the wall with relief. A moment later, the thing in the box grew quiet as well. At least its movements stopped.

Geordi looked at his friend. "We should have a plan to contain it."

Will looked around the room and found a long metal pipe. He hefted it like a baseball bat. "I've got a plan to contain it. Go ahead, lift the box."

Geordi swallowed hard, bent down, and stripped off the filthy rags. Will braced his legs and lifted the pipe over his head as Geordi grabbed the box and hoisted it up.

CHAPTER

9

Unmoving, lying on its side, the mechanical rat looked like battle debris. It had seen better days, as its fur was singed, its casing was cracked, and part of its tail-antenna was missing.

Geordi nodded to Will, and he prodded the gizmo with his length of pipe. Even when shoved around, the rat continued to look dead. *Of course,* thought Geordi, *that could be a defensive reaction.*

Outside, the battle reached its own welcome lull, and the pounding sounded dull and far away. Only the sirens continued to scream.

Geordi gazed out the small window, noting that the sky was getting dark. Whether that was due to a storm, the smoke, or the coming of night was hard to tell. The light was fading, and here they were trapped in a basement in the middle of a war zone.

But they weren't alone—they had two curious toys to keep them company, the robot and the phase modulator. Geordi glanced at the cryptic readouts on the modulator, and he made a mental note of the frequency that shut down the robot.

Then he screwed up his courage, reached down, and grabbed the furry critter. It was hot to the touch, but not so hot that he couldn't hold it. The robot smelled of burned-out rotors, gears, and gyro-servos.

"I'd say this thing has seen hard duty," said Geordi. "And you kicking it across the room into a puddle didn't do it much good."

"Too bad," said Will with satisfaction.

Geordi turned the robot over, plucked out some fake hairs, and studied the bottom panel. There were strange patterns etched in the metal. He couldn't read the patterns, but there were serial numbers that he recognized.

"This is a Federation patent number," he said. "A Federation world made this reconnaissance robot."

"Who?"

Geordi peered closely at the strange etchings. "I'm not a linguist. I can't tell more without opening it up. Maybe some of the chips are marked by point of origin. If we had the time and equipment, we could analyze the programming and find a signature that way."

"Let's make sure we take it with us," said Will. "It might be useful to show Starfleet, if we ever get home alive."

Suddenly the thing sprang to life in Geordi's hands.

Its little wheels skidded off his palms, causing sharp burns, and he yelped and dropped it. The robot hit the floor on its back and took a second to roll over.

But that was a second too long, as Will brought the pipe down on the robot with a resounding crunch. The rat shot sparks for a few seconds, then it lay still. This time it really looked dead.

Geordi shook his head sadly. "I'm sorry you had to do that."

"I'm not," said Will. "I don't trust that thing."

Geordi picked up the mechanical rat. This time its innards were rattling around, which was not a good sign. It probably had squeaked its last. He tucked the robot inside his dirty dress uniform and picked up his Coridan phase modulator.

"We can't stay down here forever," said Geordi.

"No," agreed Will. He tapped his commbadge. "Riker to *Gallant*. Riker to *Gallant*."

"Give it up," said Geordi. "I've been trying that every fifteen minutes. It doesn't work."

Will shrugged and tapped it again. "Riker to Captain Webb. Riker to Webb."

"Riker, Webb here!" came a voice that crackled with static. "The *Gallant* had to leave orbit, but most of us are okay and accounted for. Find shelter, and await further orders."

"Yes, sir," answered Will. "La Forge is with me."

"Good. Are either of you seriously injured?"

"No, sir."

"Keep a low profile and await my orders. Webb out."

With a worried frown, Will picked up his trombone. "I guess it's dangerous in orbit, too."

Geordi sat down on the dirty floor. "Is this shelter? Should we just stay here, or go somewhere else?"

Will started to speak, but he was drowned out by a sizzling sound, like bacon frying. He and Geordi whirled around to see a neon green beam come slicing through the little window, cutting the floor in half. The beam plowed up debris like an invisible bulldozer.

The cadets were caught in the half of the room nearest the staircase, and they stumbled out the door and clambered up the rubble. They had to claw their way through debris, and it was hard to keep their instruments from getting crushed.

Geordi looked up to see a sleek aircraft floating above their heads. It was about the size of a canoe. It raked the building with its deadly beam, and debris started to rain down. He and Will staggered up the stairs and ran for their lives into the open street.

The aircraft seemed to take notice of them for the first time, and it banked around and swept after them. How did it know they were in the basement? wondered Geordi. There was no time to ponder this question with death swooping down.

He and Will jumped into a crater just as the aircraft fired a volley directly at them. The shot was high, but it blasted a storefront and showered the street with bits of molten glass. The craft dipped lower to get a better angle, and Geordi could feel its sights homing in.

From nowhere a phaser blast sheered the aircraft's bow, and a chunk of it went flying off. The craft spun out of control and nearly crashed. Somehow it righted itself at the last moment and chopped off a delicate turret as it zoomed away.

The pilot was good, thought Geordi, *and he would live to fight another day. But why was he trying to kill them?*

Still panting for breath, Geordi turned and waved gratefully at the Orions. But they were already falling back and didn't seem to know that he and Will were there. To them, it was just a lucky shot taken in the middle of a retreat, but it had saved the cadet's lives.

The sky was turning into rose-colored twilight made more spectacular by the acrid smoke. Soon it would be night, which didn't bother Geordi much, as he could see well in the dark. But the rest of the cadets would be at a disadvantage in the darkness.

It made him long for those double suns of Pacifica. The thrilling music, the competition, the beach and the roller coaster—all of that seemed so long ago, and it was only yesterday. He looked up and decided that the gloom in the clouds could only be the onset of night.

With a groan, Will rolled over and looked at him. "What now?"

"Find shelter and await orders."

Will sat up and looked around the shallow crater. "Where can you get shelter on this crazy planet? If you're indoors, the buildings fall on you. If you're outdoors, the fighters strafe you."

"Then let's go someplace in between," said Geordi. "Let's find a building that has mostly fallen down but still has some walls for cover."

"And let's get there soon," said Will, glancing upward, "it's getting dark."

The cadets dragged themselves to their feet and crouched down, expecting the sky to erupt with fighters. When calm prevailed, Geordi looked for the lowest skyline and headed in that direction. He and Will jogged as fast as they could while jumping over the craters and debris.

It was odd to be running through a desolate city at twilight, looking for a bombed-out building. There was no shortage of decrepit structures to choose from, but most of them looked too dangerous.

Geordi finally found exactly what he was looking for—a building which had been sheared in half between the first and second floors. Most of the first-story walls stood intact, but the roof and ceiling were gone. It would give them some cover, but they wouldn't be crushed by falling debris.

He motioned to Will, who followed him through a breach in the wall. Geordi knew he should have been more cautious, but he was getting nervous running in the middle of the street. He felt too vulnerable, too much in the open.

Geordi kicked away some rubble to make himself a place to sit, then he slumped against the wall. He found that he was in a very long shadow, and he noted that the sun was setting behind him. He looked up at the sky and saw the dark clouds swirling angrily.

Will stumbled in after him. After he found a place to set his trumpet, he collapsed. "It's not Pacifica," he wheezed, "but it will do."

Geordi took stock of their so-called shelter. They were vulnerable on the starboard side of the building, where the wall was crumbling. Still, it was comforting to look up and see the sky, and look around and see walls.

Looking at the sky gave him hope that the *Gallant* would return and they would be rescued. Until then, it was back to survival instincts. His instincts told him to stay put for now, and hope for the best.

Will gazed at the sky and smiled wistfully. "I always thought I wanted to join Starfleet because I love adventure. But I'd rather be taking that propulsion exam right now."

Geordi chuckled. "That is Stevenson's Corollary. When you're in your armchair, you'd rather be having an adventure. When you're having an adventure, you'd rather be in your armchair."

With that thought in mind, Geordi yawned and dozed off for a moment. Actually it was hard for him to know if he was awake or asleep, because both states were unreal. He had a dream for a moment of Elofim when it had been vibrant and full of people living, not dying.

However, the people of Elofim had an arrogant streak. They had challenged their neighbors over minor affairs, and their neighbors had ganged up on them. Now the original inhabitants were defeated and long gone, and the victors fought among themselves for the spoils. Without much risk, they hired faceless mercenaries to keep the conflict going.

Geordi bolted upright from his dream, wondering how he knew so much, in such clear detail. On impulse he reached into his tunic and took out the robotic rat. Had the thing somehow affected his mind?

Then he looked at the Coridan phase modulator. He knew barely ten percent of what the alien device was capable of doing. What if it really *did* affect brain waves on a subliminal level?

It had already communicated with the robot, that was clear. What if it was *still* communicating with the robot? Stranger yet, what if the modulator was then communicating with Geordi?

He shook his head. What if he was just dreaming? That was a more likely explanation. Geordi glanced at Will and saw his friend was in a similar stupor, trying to keep his eyes open.

He was about to drift back to sleep when he heard the tromp of footsteps. It sounded like a parade, minus the drummers and instruments. Geordi sat up now, and so did Will. They looked around at the crumbling walls which surrounded them, and suddenly they didn't feel so safe.

Geordi chanced to look out of the hole they had crawled through to reach this refuge. Marching down the center of the street was a column of Orion soldiers. They picked their way through the rubble, but they didn't mind being seen. They were definitely on a mission.

In fact, they looked as if they were headed straight for Geordi and Will's hideout.

That had to be a coincidence, thought Geordi, like the wild shot that had saved their lives. But where were the Orions going so boldly?

He ducked back into the building and slumped against the wall. Will had been standing on some rubble, peering over the top of the wall, and he dropped down into a crouch.

"I don't think they've seen us," whispered Will. "What do you think they'll do?"

Geordi shrugged. "They seem to be going some-where. They'll probably march right past us."

"Yeah," said Will with relief. "Besides, they're on our side, right? We entertained them."

"That was a great concert," Geordi sighed. "We took them out of this war for a while."

He was startled when he heard orders being barked in the street. The stomping footsteps stopped abruptly, and there was the clack of machinery.

Geordi didn't want to poke his head out again, but he had no choice. It sounded as if the Orion soldiers were making camp in the street, directly in front of their hiding place. That might not be a bad thing, unless they attracted hordes of deadly aircraft.

Again Geordi inched out of his hole to try to find out what was going on. To his horror, he saw Orions setting a half dozen weapons on tripods. They were aimed directly at the cadets' hiding place!

Geordi scurried backward, slumped against the wall, and gasped, "They're about to open fire on us! We've got to get out of here!"

Will bounced to his feet, but it was too late as the first phaser blast cut a diagonal path through the wall. The cadets dropped to their stomachs as the beam slashed through the building. It leveled the wall behind them.

"Hold your fire!" shouted Geordi, but his words were drowned out by more phaser fire, followed by a photon grenade, and a thunderous explosion. Geordi curled into a ball as the Orion forces opened fire upon their crumbling shelter.

CHAPTER

10

"Why us?" cried Will as the Orions blasted away. He grabbed his trombone and hugged it to his chest.

The question hit Geordi like a slap in the face. *Why us?* What had brought them here? And what had brought the deadly aircraft after them?

There was only one answer. Geordi reached into his tunic and pulled out the furry robot. With no time to think, he jumped to his feet and tossed the gizmo as far as he could. Then he hit the dirt as the assault on their position continued.

Suddenly the wilting fire stopped and there came a flurry of new orders. Geordi heard the machinery and the footsteps moving briefly, and then the dreadful beams arced across the night sky. He covered his head, but this time the phasers and photon grenades were directed elsewhere.

The building beside them took thunderous hits. It was demolished in a few seconds. That was where Geordi had thrown the robot.

Will grabbed his sleeve and pointed toward the open spaces behind them. Where there had once been a wall was now a chalky outline. "Let's get out of here," he whispered.

They picked up their instruments and padded out the back. Without saying a word, they ran at least two kilometers, just trying to put distance between themselves and the Orion troops. Geordi really did feel as if they were caught in the crossfire—they had been fired at by both sides.

Will held up his hand and staggered to a stop. "What did you do back there?"

Geordi gasped for breath. "I threw that stupid robot away. The Orions must have detected it, and they were homing in to destroy it."

"Some souvenir," muttered Riker. "Sorry I suggested we take it along."

Geordi shrugged. "It wasn't your fault. I would have taken it, anyway." He shook his head in amazement. "Look at us, dragging our musical instruments through a war zone."

Will hefted his trombone. "They probably think *this* is a Klingon disruptor."

Geordi chuckled, then he shifted back to uneasy attention. He looked around at their present surroundings, a hilly part of town that had winding roads and the ruins of several large houses. They weren't safe yet, but the hills offered some escape routes from the low-flying aircraft.

"Geordi," said Will nervously. "We've got company again."

He turned to see about a dozen Orion soldiers come running or limping down the hill. They were pursued by one of the aircraft, but it had to swerve upward to avoid plowing into the opposite hill. The Orions took that opportunity to duck into the ragged bushes along the sides of the road.

Geordi looked at Will, and the two of them ran as fast as they could in the opposite direction. They soon found themselves climbing a hill out in the open, and Geordi became nervous again. He heard the whine of an engine in his head, but he didn't know if it was real or imaginary.

"Get in the bushes," he barked.

Will glanced at him, then remembered other times that he had been right. Both of them dropped to the pavement and rolled into the bushes.

The aircraft soared across the hill, but it didn't open fire. It seemed to be moving on. The cadets lay still with brambles sticking them in the back for several minutes, until they were sure the fighting had moved on. Breathing again, Geordi crawled out of their hiding place. He sat on the hillside and fired up the Coridan phase modulator.

"Geordi," said Will, "what do you think you're

doing? We can't take time out to play any music now. We've got to escape!"

"To where?" asked Geordi. "There is no shelter, unless we can create it. This is just a little experiment—it won't take long."

He started playing the modulator in the frequencies which had controlled the robotic rat. He was pleased to find that he could shift around and overlap signals with ease. Geordi finally had an "ear" for the modulator, as musicians would say. Only it didn't involve the ear.

He knew he was communicating with something out there, just as a musician knows he has reached an audience.

"You're going to get us killed," warned Will. "You know, the Orions are homing in on these signals, and so are the aircraft."

"You wanted to get them talking, didn't you?" asked Geordi.

"Through a musical instrument?"

Geordi shrugged. "Why not? Music hath charms to soothe the savage breast. This is music I can't hear, but I can *feel* it through this instrument. I don't use my senses in a typical way, so maybe I'm more attuned to this."

Suddenly there was a strange squeaking sound, and Geordi saw movement in the shadows around him. The scraggly shrubbery by the side of the road began to twitch and jerk. Will raised his trombone like a weapon and stepped back.

"Stop playing," ordered Will.

Geordi held his hands up. "I stopped already." He looked down at the phase modulator, wondering exactly what he had been doing. It was as if his playing wasn't his own—but a collaboration between himself, the modulator, the audience, and his subconscious mind.

He turned the machine off, then he looked up to see a huge pack of rodents, snakes, and frogs come hopping and slithering out of the bushes.

"Whoa, Geordi!" said Will, backing up. "What did you do?"

"I guess I'm the Pied Piper," answered Geordi. "I seem to be speaking their language."

"Then tell them to go away!" said Will nervously. He turned around to run in the opposite direction, but the robotic menagerie were closing in from both sides.

"Why so many?" muttered Will.

"The enemy must have just released them," said Geordi. "Maybe it's in preparation for a big strike. They're perfect for reconnaissance and picking targets. No wonder the Orions are low on morale—how can they fight these things?"

"Can you put them all to sleep?" asked Will.

Geordi looked worriedly at the army of crawling robots. They were not moving, just waiting in eerie silence. "Putting them to sleep would be taking sides in the conflict."

"You said they were made by a Federation world. So that would mean that the Prime Directive doesn't apply! Both of these sides are already at our level of technology."

"That's true." Geordi looked at the phase modulator in his hands. By accident, he had stumbled upon a way to communicate with one of the warring factions. Could he turn the tide in battle? How important were these tiny robots?

"They're trying to kill us, aren't they?" asked Geordi.

Will nodded. "They sure are. And if you won't put them to sleep, you've got to throw the phase modulator away. Or it's going to get us killed."

Geordi turned on the instrument. "What if this backfires?"

"Geordi," said Will, "everybody is trying to kill us now! How can things get any worse?"

The cadet nodded somberly and looked at his audience of fake rodents and reptiles. A green and orange snake curled up by his feet waited patiently. He took a deep breath and plied the colorful buttons, taking up where he had left off.

At once he felt the strange feedback he had noticed before, a feeling of comfort and satisfaction. Several of the rodents fell to their sides and looked as dead as the first one. Of course, remembered Geordi, the first one had come alive again.

He continued to play until all the tiny robots became inactive. Geordi faded out by decreasing the power, and he finally ended the second concert on Elofim that day. He watched the robots nervously, waiting to see if they would reawaken. But they remained still and unmoving.

"Good job," whispered Will. "At least we can get away from them. Let's go."

Gripping their instruments, Geordi and Will tiptoed through the sleeping sea of rats and reptiles. Geordi glanced over his shoulder, wondering if their actions could have any effect on the war. A bunch of reconnaissance robots couldn't affect the war that much, could they?

He tried to stop thinking about the Prime Directive. Their orders were to seek shelter. Since there was no safe zone, they would have to create their own shelter. That wasn't a misuse of technology, only a matter of survival.

When they got about thirty meters beyond the circle of robots, Will stopped and considered the twisting streets. "Where to?"

"We don't want to get lost," said Geordi. "We want the captain to be able to find us. Let's make our way back to the place we gave the concert."

Will shrugged. "I don't like that idea, but I can't think of a better one." He pointed his trombone down the closest street and marched off.

Geordi followed his friend, although he was feeling increasingly uneasy again. The sirens were a dull throb in the distance, and the heavy explosions were even farther off. Still he hugged his phase modulator tightly to his chest.

Night didn't usually bother him, but this one did. He wanted to crouch down and wait for daylight, but they were better off to keep moving. So far, every time they had stopped they had been attacked.

He glanced again over his shoulder. That was when he saw it—the telltale vapor trail high above the clouds!

The aircraft was coming their way, closing ground quickly.

"Will!" shouted Geordi. "Aircraft right behind us, dropping in altitude."

Will whirled around. "How many?"

"Just one." Geordi dashed off the street and crouched down in the thin shrubbery.

"Maybe it will fly over us," suggested Will.

Geordi studied the sky, waiting for the deadly craft to break through the cloud cover. With his VISOR, he could see the vapor trail plus a smaller plasma trail in front of it. That was odd, and he wondered if it could be some other kind of craft.

Like an arrow, the fighter sliced through the clouds and shot straight toward them. Geordi gasped. Now he knew where the plasma stream was coming from—it shot from a hole in the craft's nose cone. This was the same ship that had tried to kill them before!

"Run!" shouted Geordi. He jumped over the shrubs and ran until the ground suddenly disappeared beneath him. With a yell, Geordi tumbled down a hill covered with brambles and debris. He wrapped his arms protectively around the phase modulator and tried to stop himself with his legs.

He finally bounced to a rough stop next to the crumbling wall of a house. As he tried to regain his senses, a beam shot across the night sky and obliterated the hill where he and Will had been standing. Clods of dirt rained down upon him, and Geordi scrambled to his feet.

"Will!" he shouted. "Will Riker!"

There was no answer. Frightened, Geordi lifted his head to see the aircraft making a wide bank in the night sky. It doubled back, slowed to hover speed, and strafed the hill with its lethal rays.

Debris poured down upon Geordi, but he dragged himself to his feet. Keeping his head low, he tried to run. A ferocious explosion knocked him off his feet, and the entire hill erupted in flame!

Geordi shook his head and tried to face his enemy, but the flames were like a furnace. The craft must have blasted open an underground fuel tank! He stumbled backward, hoping the fire would spoil the pilot's aim.

But the deadly beam kept coming. It cut a path of flame down the hillside, straight toward Geordi!

CHAPTER

11

Geordi dodged to his left, but the beam changed direction and kept coming. Wherever he went, the craft adjusted its aim and the lethal ray drew closer.

Suddenly from high on the hill came the most horrible noise of all—a blaring trombone at full volume. It sounded like a herd of dying moose as it blared over and over again. The aircraft reversed course and headed to investigate.

Geordi gazed up the hillside and could see a furtive figure dashing among the flames. Will had given him a few more seconds of life, and he had better put it to good use. Will was right about the phase modulator— he had better do something with it, or throw it out.

Geordi turned the device on and began to play, trying to relax his tense, nervous muscles. He began with
the frequencies that had controlled the tiny robots, and
then he let his subconscious mind take over. He envi-
sioned himself playing directly to the aircraft with the
hole in its nose, the one that was trying to kill him.

He was sure that the ground-based robots were communicating with the aircraft, plus the Orions knew how
to jam them. So he should be able to connect, too.
Geordi plied the colorful keys of the phase modulator,
and he knew that he was connecting.

Sleep, he tried to tell the aircraft. Even though
Geordi felt confident, he was still afraid to look up.
Finally he stared into the night sky. Like a great white
shark cruising the depths, the aircraft banked through
the dark clouds and angled toward him.

Geordi caught his breath, expecting the ship to open
fire. He began to play the modulator again, trying to
coax that relaxed feedback he had experienced before.
He heard a desperate voice and clomping footsteps.

"Geordi, run!" shouted Will Riker. "It's headed back
this way!"

He tried to ignore the friend who had just saved his
life. "How far could we run?" he asked. "We have to
communicate peace, not war. Let me see if I can put
the ship to sleep."

Will looked doubtfully at the deadly craft, which was
looming closer and closer. "All right, play to it. I'll
help you."

He lifted his trombone to his lips and began to play
the solo from "Stardust," the solo he wanted so badly

to perform. Somehow Will's loyalty gave Geordi all the confidence he needed. His fingers flew over the keys, and he hit chords and resonances that felt just right.

The ship dipped even closer, as if it would kill them or be killed in the process. But it didn't open fire with its lethal rays. Will put down his trombone and just stared at the oncoming aircraft.

"I think we can run now," said Will.

Geordi gulped. "So do I."

They dashed in opposite directions, scrambling over the rubble. The aircraft whooshed past them like a meteor and plowed into the hillside! The force of the explosion knocked Geordi off his feet. It also knocked out his hearing and his vision for several seconds.

Geordi shook the dirt out of his hair and concentrated on getting his vision back. This had happened so many times now, he was getting used to it. Maybe one day he would learn to keep his VISOR working through even the most desperate actions.

When his vision returned, Geordi looked up to see the aircraft buried in solid dirt. A few sparks crackled along its fuselage, and he worried about the ship bursting into flames. Luckily the dirt acted as a dampening agent, and the sparks sputtered out.

As Geordi approached the stricken aircraft, he was amazed at how dead it looked. It was like a war relic—an old cannon in a Civil War fort. Will was a few meters ahead of him, and he crouched down to study the rear thrusters.

"Accelerated plasma drive engines," said Will. "Think I'll pass that propulsion exam?"

"You have a good excuse if you don't," said Geordi. "You know, that's a common Federation design."

"So what else is new?" Will climbed over a pile of steaming dirt to inspect the cockpit. "Do you think anybody is alive?"

Geordi also climbed over the dirt and peered into the cockpit. He wasn't surprised to find that the craft had no pilot. It was just a mass of instruments built on top of a plasma coil.

"It's a drone," he said. "All run by computer. After I played to it, I was beginning to suspect it was just a machine."

Will's face twisted into anger. "So this stupid war has mercenaries fighting robots! Over a dead planet. Well, that's just great. I say we put an end to this right now."

"We can't," said Geordi, "until we see who built this craft. Get a pipe and help me crack open this windshield."

"With pleasure," answered Will.

Five minutes later, they had broken into the enemy ship, and Geordi was studying the instruments by the light of his modulator. He noticed a plaque at the bottom of one panel; he spit at it and wiped it off with his sleeve.

"Tellarite," said Geordi with amazement. "I recognize that symbol from the boxes Leshelle used when he was packing to go home."

"Yeah," said Will, "and Tellar is the closest Federation planet to Elofim. Could this be what made Leshelle quit the academy?"

"He said blood was thicker than mud. Maybe somebody in his family is connected with this war."

Will nodded thoughtfully. "Maybe he was afraid that the war would be discovered. You know, I wonder if Jaktu brought the band here just so we would find out about the war."

"I thought about that, too," said Geordi. "I think Jaktu felt sorry for his troops."

They were silent for a moment, then Will spoke. "Now we can do whatever we want to defend ourselves. Is there anything in this ship we can use?"

Geordi gazed down at the instrument panel. "I think I can patch the phase modulator into the drone's communications system. In effect, we can issue orders to all the drones at once. What should I play? I mean, tell them?"

"Surrender," said Will. "Total surrender."

"Shouldn't we contact Captain Webb first?"

"No, let's make sure it works before we tell anyone to come out of cover. Do you think Captain Webb would be against a ceasefire?"

"No, I don't think so," said Geordi.

They patched the phase modulator into the drone's comm panel, hoping they would contact hundreds of aircraft at once. Geordi played for over an hour, broadcasting the same persistent message of peace and surrender.

They didn't know whether the message had gotten through until they heard the wild cheers of the Orion soldiers. A band of them came tearing down the hill, weeping their hearts out with joy.

They rushed up to Geordi and Will and nearly crushed them with bear hugs. Then they moved on, tears rolling down their grimy green faces. Geordi finally turned the phase modulator off.

Will smiled at him. "Good playing, Geordi. You can be in my band anytime."

"Thanks."

Will's commbadge beeped, and he tapped it. "Riker here."

"This is Captain Webb. I don't know if you're aware of it, but the enemy forces have surrendered. I think we're safe to leave now."

Will gave Geordi a sheepish grin. "We know about it, sir. In fact, it's not a real surrender—we arranged it. La Forge hooked up his Coridan phase modulator to a downed aircraft, and we ordered all the aircraft to surrender. I hope we didn't overstep our bounds."

Webb breathed a sigh of relief. "I'll worry about that when we're safely back at Starfleet Academy. I always knew that phase modulator would come in handy! Until then, thank you for your quick actions."

The captain cleared his throat. "Captain Webb to all members of the Starfleet Academy Band. Hostilities have ceased, and I am happy to say we are all accounted for. I've contacted the *Gallant*, and she'll need a few minutes to get into position. Stand by to transport in approximately ten minutes. Webb out."

Geordi and Will cut loose with their own cheers. Then Geordi glanced back at the drone aircraft, which was now part of the landscape. He wondered how many Orions it had killed before meeting its fate as a pile of junk.

* * *

Three days later, Will Riker was charging across the commons of Starfleet Academy, and Geordi was racing after him. A blustery wind seemed to force him back, and he finally had to tug on Will's sleeve.

"Stop, will you!" demanded Geordi. "Can't we walk to Captain Webb's office?"

Will turned angrily on him. "Only if you promise not to talk to me. I'm quitting the band, and that's all there is to it!"

"Come on," pleaded Geordi. "Not all of our road trips are like that one. Most of them are calm and peaceful."

"I was going to quit even before it got crazy," Will insisted. "They snubbed me, they pulled practical jokes on me, and I nearly got killed! Those are all good reasons to quit the band, as far as I'm concerned." He stalked off toward the science building.

Geordi caught up with him as he entered the lift, and Will scowled at his friend. "And do you know what? I just got a B-minus on that propulsion exam. I couldn't even get a break because of our adventure! That's it! I'm finished with this band. Floor three."

The lift doors closed and whisked them away to the third floor. "That's not a bad grade," said Geordi. "We have lots of admirals who couldn't do as well."

Will looked pointedly at him. "I'm quitting, Geordi, that's all there is to it. These people will never be nice to me. Maybe I'll form my own band."

The lift doors opened, and Geordi followed Will across the corridor into Captain Webb's office. The ensign who served as his aide ushered them past her cubicle. "He's waiting for you, gentlemen."

She actually smiled, which was a first for Geordi. Even Will slowed down as they entered the inner chamber. They were both surprised by the number of people in Webb's office. In addition to the band director, there was Commander Baxter, Akusta, Stinson, and several more upperclassmen.

The portly captain rose to his feet and held out his hand. "Cadet La Forge, Cadet Riker, welcome! I apologize for the informal nature of this gathering, but I will explain."

"Captain Webb," said Will, "I have something I want to say."

The captain smiled. "I'll give you time to make a speech, if you like, but first let me bring everyone up to date. Owing to the Tellarite involvement, the Federation has acted quickly to clear up matters on Elofim.

"The Tellarite government was not directly involved. The real warring parties, the Riquatru and the Hakshos, used to be allies. They worked together to defeat the native people of Elofim, then they turned on each other. That's why they resorted to robots and mercenaries to do their fighting."

Geordi leaned forward, listening intently. The information he had gotten in his dream was true!

Webb continued, "As you suggested, we contacted Leshelle, and he told us about his uncle, an arms dealer who sold weapons to the Riquatru. The Hakshos hired the Orions.

"The Riquatru assumed that the war would be over

quickly, but the Orion mercenaries fought better than expected. So they stepped up the fighting, and that's when Jaktu brought us in. Jaktu is dead, by the way."

"We know," said Geordi. "We think he brought us there to stop the war."

Webb nodded grimly. "He would be happy to know that all the Orion soldiers have been sent home. The Federation will arbitrate a settlement between the warring parties. The Tellarite government will pay to rebuild the planet."

Geordi looked puzzled. "And the people who once lived on Elofim?"

The captain shook his head. "If any survived, they are scattered all over the galaxy. We will try to include them in the talks."

Will raised his hand impatiently. "Captain Webb, may I say something?"

"Yes, after one more announcement." The captain gave them a jovial smile. "La Forge, Riker, we would love to publicly commend you for your bravery under fire. But part of the agreement with the Tellarites is that we do not embarrass them. But we have our own ways to honor you."

He turned to Geordi and presented him with a stack of music charts. "You're no longer a roadie, La Forge. From now on, you're a full member of the band, with all privileges. We'll write parts for you and the phase modulator."

Akusta grinned. "That means first on the transporter."

"Congratulations, La Forge," said Commander Baxter.

Geordi accepted the music charts with his mouth agape. "I can't believe this, thank you."

Even Will Riker was forced to smile. "Geordi, you deserve it. As for me . . ."

"As for you," said Captain Webb, "the band has its own honor. Mr. Stinson, go ahead."

Stinson stepped forward and ran his hand over his shaven head. "Riker, you stood up to us, which is something we don't usually like. But in your case, we'll make an exception. We've got a concert here on campus in two weeks, and we voted. You're going to play the solo on 'Stardust.' "

Will stared at him. "The solo! Really? This isn't a joke, is it?"

"We don't joke about the solo," said Akusta. "Once you've played the solo, you're a veteran. No more jokes."

"All right, Riker," said Captain Webb. "You've been wanting to make a speech, so here's your chance. What have you got to say?"

Geordi looked expectantly at his friend. Could Will quit the band right after receiving the ultimate honor? It wouldn't be the same without him.

Will finally smiled and shook his head. "I just wanted to say that next year, we're going to win that competition on Pacifica!"

Cheers echoed in Captain Webb's office.

About the Author

JOHN VORNHOLT was born in Marion, Ohio, and knew he wanted to write science fiction when he discovered Doc Savage novels and the words of Edgar Rice Burroughs. But somehow he wrote nonfiction and television scripts for many years, including animated series such as *Dennis the Menace, Ghostbusters,* and *Super Mario Brothers.* He was also an actor and playwright, with several published plays to his credit.

John didn't get back to his first love—writing SF—until 1989 with the publication of his first Star Trek Next Generation novel, *Masks.* He wrote two more, *Contamination* and *War Drums;* a classic Trek novel, *Sanctuary;* and a Deep Space Nine novel, *Antimatter.* For young readers, he's also written two other Starfleet Academy books, *Capture the Flag* and *Aftershock,* plus *The Tale of the Ghost Riders,* an "Are You Afraid of the Dark?" book. All of these titles are available from Pocket Books.

John is also the author of several nonfiction books for kids and the novel *The Witching Well.*

John lives in Tucson, Arizona, with his wife, Nancy, his children, Sarah and Eric, and his dog, Bessie.